The Bloody Curse of Humankind

Other books that are written by Ashaki Boelter:

Doomed School
Beware of a Cat's Fury
The Nok
Witch Momma, Dummy for Hire
Destined To Win
Eagle Tripping
The Thirst for Blood

The Bloody Curse of Humankind

A Novel

Ashaki Boelter

Shakalot High Entertainment

The Bloody Curse of Humankind

Copyright © 2020 by Ashaki Boelter

Ashaki Boelter
Sacramento, California

Library of Congress

Cataloging-in-Publication Data

ISBN: 978-1-7358905-2-4

All illustrations © by Ashaki Boelter

Cover by
Printed in the USA by
Lulu Enterprise
3131 RDU Center, Suite 210
Morrisville, NC 27560

Published by Shakalot High Entertainment
Edited In-House Shakalot High
Shakalot High Entertainment books may be ordered through various online booksellers

Dedicated to my close friends and family

Table of Contents

"And many of them that sleep in the dust of the earth shall awake, some to everlasting life, and some to shame and everlasting contempt." (King James Version Bible, Daniel 12:2)

NOT suitable for children due to references to drugs, language, sex, and adult themes.

Chapter 1
The Contract

Windy gusts ascended from the busy town below and into the sealed windows of Marshall Canny Corporation offices atop the western hills of Portland. Although operations were ceased for the unusually sunny holiday weekend, an accountant named Alvin Snow was authorized overtime to study recent deficiencies discovered in the company's accounting records.

After Alvin calculated ledger totals using mathematical formulas and dissected equations and numbers from several ledgers, he discovered that the company's budget was full of ambiguities. He snapped another pencil across the desk in dire frustration and tiresome because he also found that there were boundless errors if calculation and input throughout the company's last three quarters! He stood to his feet to take a break, but he needed to check in with the company's CEO, David Snyder, by phone, if he found any discrepancy or a possibility of embezzlement.

It was a big deal! Someone in accounting had stolen from the company's gains before it was reported. Together, Mr. Snyder and Alvin riddled through many questionable and inept calculations in the financial ledgers. It wasn't until Mr. Snyder brought in a particular thug, a retired mathematical genius of a former mob named Stephen Brady, to figure it all out. After all, nobody screwed with Mr. Snyder's money and got away with it. Crimes that involved theft with his money either ended with jail time or a life-long, jaw paralysis, missing teeth, and missing fingers.

All three of them came to hypotheses and a near conclusion. The bookkeeper, Denny Brown, falsified many pages by not including all receipts of donation or for items sold. Every receipt had a confirmation number on it, which were generated and recorded in a separate, hidden backup database that was off-campus.

"I think that we can take it from here," said Mr. Snyder. He thanked Alvin for his hard work and dismissed him for the rest of the holiday weekend. He was proud to have hired Alvin, but he and his heavy wanted the primary bookkeeper in the office at once, whom they deemed responsible for the blunder.

Within an hour, to their propitious request, the bookkeeper joined them in a conference to discuss hapless incompetency.

"Denny Brown, I am glad you made it here." The CEO pointed to a chair. "Please, have a seat."

"While I appreciate your extension of courtesy, I am on short time being that it is the weekend. I have parental duties today; I need to pick up my children from daycare. Can you make this quick?"

"Denny, my sincerest apologies; I'll make this quick," replied Mr. Snyder. "This inquiry of you is of utmost importance."

"And who may I ask is the jacked gentleman behind you?"

The CEO smiled. "This is a financial specialist and a retired auditor, among many other talents, that I hired to go over your ledgers. His name is Stephen Brady, but that's of little consequence."

"You're a big fellow," said Denny. He figured that the retired auditor was more than a savvy, numbers nerd. "You must eat a lot of cheese and drink a lot of milk to be that big."

The CEO's guest bit his lip and popped his knuckles. "I'm lactose intolerant."

"Let me get to the chase," said Mr. Snyder. "Over the last three quarters, Denny, there were many inconsistencies in your calculations throughout a host of unwarranted deductions. So before we submit our information to the government, I wanted a closer look."

"Mr. Snyder and Mr. Brady, please, pardon my eluding behavior," said Denny, "but this is preposterous. Those numbers are correct; I've checked them, forward and backward!"

Mr. Brady sucked down shreds of lunch meat between his two front teeth. Then he spoke, "The reason we called you here was to let you know that we found where you secretly directed some of this company's profit to an off-shore bank account of yours, directing this company to report a profit loss for millions of dollars! Upon further investigation, you also took advantage of the profit losses by doing insider trading."

Denny raised his arms in disagreement. "You're insane!"

"Go on and call the police, Mr. Snyder." The hired heavy grabbed his briefcase and readied to leave. "He's lucky that you didn't pay me enough to off this scum. I hate liars."

"Wait a minute!" Denny shouted.

"You've made a lot of money," stated Mr. Snyder. He picked up the office phone and began to dial the sheriff directly. "I was able to trace diverted deposits to an off-shore bank account under your name. As it turns out, Denny, you're a very wealthy man, and you're going to jail. Congratulations. In the meantime, you can call your children a ride-share or a cab to get home."

"I am afraid that I will not do that," answered Denny. He pulled a pistol from his back pocket and fired a bullet into the buffed financial specialist's head that also dropped his concealed gun!

Mr. Brady dropped dead behind the CEO. The phone dangled from Mr. Snyder's hand with a busy signal, as he had not wholly dialed the police phone number.

"You certainly are a piece of work, Denny?"

"Hang up the phone," ordered Denny. He juked his gun at the CEO as if he was going to pull the trigger. "You and I are going to do a little business, so sit there and shut your mouth. You keep your hands where I can see them, or your fate will be similar to the dead muscle-head that you hired."

"Now, let's be reasonable, Denny."

"I knew you would eventually catch on, being the greedy billionaire you are. Mr. Snyder, or if I may call you David if you would have only done your research, and not wasted time on the ledgers or at the golf course, you would have found that your plan to rattle me was dangerous."

"Who do you think you are? You're an accountant that makes pennies and drives a bucket! I asked you a question!"

"How else would I have known, David, that you'd hire Mr. Brady? I have done my research, and you're as easy to predict just from your previous handlings. I know about all the undisclosed and unlawful dealing of yours. Let's just say that word of mouth gets around in the circle I mingle with nowadays."

"Cut the crap, Denny! You're going to jail!" The CEO pointed to the cameras throughout the room. "You don't know anything, and you don't scare me! You're bluffing me, and even if you blow me away, the police and I are the only ones authorized to get the footage from the private and guarded software!"

"Nobody is going to get arrested," replied Denny. "I know that there is no darn way you're turning his dead body over to authorities. It would incriminate you and how you're connected to members of such distinguished mobs, past, and present. And there is no way that I'm dying today."

"You won't get away with this! I know a lot of people, and the man you killed has ties to a lot of the mob still!"

"Oh, I'm so scared," replied Denny. "Unlike your actions in our lengthy company meetings, can you please shut up? You see, with the wealth I have now, from the money I stole from you, I run this place! Poor Mr. Snyder's old constituents now work for me! Had he not retired and kept up on who's who, he would've known I was in charge now. And if you had done your research, you would've heard about me running this town."

"Spit it out and stop wasting my time, you prick. You haven't killed me yet, so you must want something from me."

"You have been a lonely man since the death of your wife," said Denny, who dropped his pistol to his side. "I've known you for many years; I know that you're a smart businessman, Dave. That's why I figure you will be smart and sign over the $700 million Woodland Yards property to me. That's what I want."

"Get the hell out of here. Are you serious? No!"

"Come on, David. I'm not a murderer. I'm a businessman. Some of my lawyers and I recently got together; we have come up with a form for you to sign. Here, you are. You can read over it in your own spare time. I just need your signature down on the line."

"No, I will not do so!"

Denny Brown slammed his fist on the desk. "You old stubborn fool, I have a gun with a bullet, and your name on it pointed at your old ass. You must be incredibly stuck-on-stupid not to sign this contract, or you're hiding something on that property that is worth your life and suddenly very valuable to me."

"The greed of man is far less dangerous than what lurks inside that property. I shall not sign this contract!"

"You've had control of that property for over twenty years, and you won't do anything with it!" Denny realized that he was probably going to have to blow the CEO away and forge the signature. His crooked attorneys rejected that provocation for such an acquisition unless it was the only method of madness left.

"No, I will not sign the land over to you and your constituents."

"I have worked for you for over twenty years, David! I do not want to shoot you. That property just sits there rotting and is one of our city's ugliest eyesores. Allow me to take that off of your hands and finally do something with it; it'll be the future's most profitable and finest sports arena! Perhaps you can invest in it later?"

David stared blankly into the hole of Denny's pistol.

"This is your last offer, sir."

The CEO chuckled. "You want to tear down that block of ruins and build a sports arena? We've already got one of those across from downtown, which hosts a pretty good basketball team, I must say. They've put us on the map already, you know, rip city!"

"They haven't won jack shit since 1977, and they've cost me a lot of betting money over forty years!"

"Hey, you need to calm down with that gun!"

"Mr. Snyder, along with an attached casino, a bar, and a high-class strip club with the world's finest women, my arena will make Portland, Oregon, one of the hottest spots in North America. Do you know how much money I'll be able to kick into this city?"

"Leave Woodland Yards alone, I beg of you!"

"Listen to me, you old bastard. You'd better sign over that property, or else I'll blow your brains out all over this office!" Denny grabbed Mr. Snyder and slammed him onto the table. The angry accountant smashed the tip of his pistol into the elderly CEO's temple!

"Inside the basement of that baron property rests... Sir Sange."

"I don't give a damn about who is buried in there! You sign this contract, or I swear to my word that your guts will drip from these walls after I blow your brains out!"

"He once rose to terrorize our town," continued the CEO. "We outsmarted the vampire magician once, but twice, he'll be aware and well-planned. Currently, he is trapped, blessed to us as mere ash under many rising sunlight of years not to be disturbed. I will not give you access to the bloody curse of humankind for as long as I live!"

"Mr. Snyder, don't you dare try to sell me on that vampire blasphemy! I've lived long enough to have heard that fable once or so. Do I look like a child to you? Pick up the pen and sign that paper, or you will not live very long!"

With a gun to his head and a pen in his hand, Mr. Snyder whispered, "The dead one has condemned itself to a waiting place nearest hell, between worlds of longstanding judgment. I beg of you not to disturb his resting place; his resurrection will be our damnation. I forbid you to continue this tyranny!"

"This is the last time I say it," said Denny. He cocked the trigger on his pistol. "Sign the papers or else, man! We go back many years, and I don't want to do it, David, but you're leaving me no choice! Pick up the pen!"

"If I sign this paper, I sign the death certificate of all men. I only pray that God helps us."

Denny watched the reluctant CEO nervously sign the contract. Suddenly, countless and imaginary dollars floated across Denny's eyes. He praised David and said, "It was a pleasure doing business with you, Mr. Snyder. And you'll not call any police if you know what's good for you. By the way, because I am now a rich man, I don't need any more of your money. I quit, you asshole!"

"What you should do is quit your plan. You're going to start something that you'll never finish. I assure you that the devil you bought will see to it."

"Whatever. Hey, I'm sorry about the bloody mess. The chunky guy you hired was a bleeder. But, do your homework the next time you want to play in my world. None of this had to go down. "

The CEO sat back in his chair and watched his ex-employee suavely walkout. He whispered, "I plead for forgiveness from the Lord, for all of the lives I have put in danger by signing that paper. The blood around Mr. Brady doesn't amount to the bloodshed becoming of the violent resurrection of the cursed soul."

Chapter 2

Build My Empire

Unlike the prior weeks of windy gusts and sprinkling rain, the radiant sun beamed amazingly upon Portland, a breath of winter warmth that uncommonly relaxed the typically depressing rainfall. It was a great day for a car wash, to hike, or to work in the field of construction.

"We got all of the homeless people out, and we're clear to tear down the ruins," said the construction foreman. He stood in attention to Denny Brown, who watched homeless people stumbling across the street with dirty sleeping bags and grocery carts. "We went through the boxes in the basement and found books of old ledgers, some garbage, and even an urn. Shall we go on and flatten everything? It appears that everybody is out, and I got an excavator operator ready to demolish this place, as we speak."

"The faster that ruin goes away, the faster I make money," replied Denny Brown. He popped the collar of his pink dress shirt and buffed rings on his fingers. He straightened his flannel grey suit coat and cleared his throat and whispered, "Well, if this vampire fable exists, good luck climbing your way out of all the rubble."

The construction foreman scratched his head. He heard Denny over the machinery engines. "I don't get it."

"It was a joke."

"Oh!" laughed the foreman. "Of course, it was. After all, there are no such things as vampires. You almost sounded convinced."

"Hey, if anything crawls out, save me on buying a tombstone and just slam a big rock onto it." Denny then puckered his lips and flared his nostrils in front of the foreman. "Do you want to get paid or not? I can find another company if you're going to quiz my intellect. Now, you instruct your men to carry on! Do you understand? I'll be over in my car if you need anything."

The foreman hollered out to his construction crew, "Alright men, let's go ahead and clear. It's time to tear the mother down!"

As soon as everybody in the crew backed away, the foreman whistled. He gave thumbs up to the man in the heaviest of machines, the giant excavator.

The rumbling machine moved forward into the ruin. The giant bucket came down on the building with a loud thud, as Dennis watched with delight. As the building fell, smoke arose from the chambers below. The taped-off area was a danger zone, as bricks and steel smashed to the earth.

Below the emerging rubble, in the basement, were boxes of expired books and items, where rodents scattered for safety. They dodged falling beams and powerless wires that whipped the floors. Oils, chemicals, and gasoline from equipment that fell from miscellaneous boxes ignited from sparking steel pieces that crashed around in the toxic smoke.

Within that blur of destruction, a crushed California myotis acrobatically dodged falling beams, but with little success of escape, eventually, got blasted across its furry head. The brain-seeped bat crashed violently into the ashes of a destroyed urn. The trapped bat squirmed and squealed in torturous terror as its blood oozed into gelatinous goo and boiled into acidic agony of the cursed. The damned ashes from the broken urn saturated the bat's displeasing blood into a frenzied feeding.

Above ground, Denny exited his car and walked to the construction area. Hours had passed, and the night became. For his dinner, he took one last bite of half a bologna sandwich and threw a mushy tomato in the street.

"Make no mistake," he told the foreman. "These are not raindrops rolling down my face. These are tears of joy!"

"It looks as if a big storm has just developed tonight," said the foreman. "We may need to put this off until tomorrow morning. I don't like the look of those dark clouds. Funny, I don't recall seeing any kind of rainstorm in the forecast."

Crackle! Crackle! Thunder and lightning struck the skies and concerned every person in the city. Strange red and grey clouds quickly devoured the starry skies for as far as the eye could see. The nightfall overcame the day at death's command in Portland.

"Heavy clouds and a sprinkle, that's all it is!" Denny declared. "This is Portland! It rains nearly three hundred days a year! Out here, we tan in the damn rain! We play soccer and go to clubs in this weather. So, no one is going home until I say so, and the job gets done! I'm paying you nitwits to do a fricking job. Do you understand? I don't care if it takes you all night, I want all of the ruins crushed to the earth right now, or else I'll find somebody else to do the job! Do you understand me, young man?"

"No worries," said the foreman. He instructed his men to continue working. He snarled at Denny, who returned to his car. "Alright, guys, you heard the boss! You all need to get back to work!"

"It's spooky out here tonight, man!" Workers shared the same consensus. Something had not felt right about the reddened and grey clouds that seemed to hum across the dark sky. "We're all scared! Why is it so reddish out here?"

"You all get your ass back to work!"

Below the smoky rubble, hidden in a space supported by leaned beams, a shadow kneeled alongside crushed furnishing and boxes. Death's eyes slowly opened and shifted over a shoulder, as his sense of smell was triggered by near, human blood.

The stranger's anger suddenly increased for being awakened yet again. His agonies, to have watched his cursed wife, at last memory, descend into the blackness at the hands of slayers and the severe cruelty he experienced at his previous demise, made him stand in the rubble with bloodthirsty rage! The sinister shadow of man metamorphosed into a dark gel and flowed into the gutter's rain and towards the luxury car that was parked across the street. There, a human stood alone.

"I'm in the money," sang Denny. He whistled a tune and pulled his key from his pants pocket. Then he closed his trunk and walked to his driver's door. Suddenly, a darker and ominous shadow overtook his vast shadow. "Whoa! You scared me, coming up on me like that in the dark! I almost put a bullet in your ass, boy."

"You're dressed up, unlike the others across the street. Are you the manager? Are you responsible for waking me?"

"I am the boss," replied Denny. "So, why don't you take your homeless, too-tall spooking ass to a shelter and stay off of my property. Now, you run along, boy!"

"I do not see any 'boys' around here."

"What? Are you Latino or something then? The streetlights are not as bright out here, so excuse me."

"I am mixed of two races," answered the tall man. "I am of black and white descent."

"Well," said Denny, "that still makes you a boy then, doesn't it. Now, run along and go play basketball down the street in the dark."

Denny turned away to unlock his car door but did not see the fangs suddenly drop from the stranger's gums. "Do you need some food or something, you spook? I will not give you any money, but I have half a bologna sandwich in my car if you want it."

"I want your blood."

Denny turned around and faced the large man. "So, that's it! Mr. Snyder wants to play childish games by trying to scare me away from the project! I'll deal with him later. For now, boy, I'm going to kick your got' damned Halloween butt."

"I told you; I do not see any 'boys' around here!"

As chunky as Denny looked, he surprisingly sucker-kicked the stranger in the mouth with lightning speed and followed it up with a cracking left hook! Though he swung so hard, had it not been for the stranger that grabbed him by the neck with one hand, he would have fallen through the pavement!

"Let go of me!" Denny was miraculously lifted from the ground with the stranger's one hand with ease. He swung and fought for his life, as he stared back into his adversary's deathly pupils, and soon realized that the vampire tale was real! Nobody witnessed what was going on outside of his car because of the construction site smoke, the fluttering dim streetlights, and noises!

"The next time you address me," said the stranger, "you address me as Sir Sange! Is that clear?"

"I'm sorry, sir! Oh, God, help me! Please, don't kill me!"

"By the way you're dressed differently from the others, you seem important. Are you in charge of that demolition across the street? I will not ask you again!"

"I am Denny Brown," answered the helpless criminal. "I acquired that property, and I am tearing it down to build my empire."

"Is that so? You could be very valuable to me," said Sange. "You'd be good to serve me until I figure some things out. In the meantime, I shall run the empire that you're now building for me."

Denny frantically pulled a gun from his dress coat and placed the tip against Sange's head. "You're wrong, you freak! That is my baby. Now, you put me down, or I will blow your brains out!"

"Aren't you convinced that your weapon will not affect me? I've lifted you from the ground without an ounce of sweat and with one arm. You cannot hurt me with your toy!"

Pop! Pop! Denny fired his pistol, as nobody heard the sounds over the construction demolition.

Sir Sange hissed with more anguish, as bullets sunk into his noggin. The holes in his head closed up as if he was never shot. Then, he spat bullets from his mouth to the ground and revealed drooling fangs! Indeed Sange was more than angered. He was infuriated.

"But you're not real!" Denny cried. "Vampires aren't real!"

"You will do my bidding," instructed Sange. Calmly, he added, "You will build my kingdom and serve me!"

"No!" Denny repeated over-and-over and finally came to terms that the tale of the immortally cursed man was real! He apologized amply for his rudeness and willingly dropped his gun, but his surrender was futile. "Please don't kill me!"

Sir Sange hurriedly pulled Denny by the neck to his salivating mouth and covered them both within his dark cape. The bloodthirsty vampire latched onto the mortal's neck like a starving serpent and vacuumed so much blood from Denny that he fell to his knees in blood-drunken exhaustion.

About an hour later, the mysteriously haunting rainfall washed away the bloodshed off the street, as the soaking foreman approached Denny's car. He hunched over and knocked on the driver window.

"Hey Mr. Brown," said the foreman, "we've finished the demolition, but I got word from the higher up that we'll have to continue the project after this windy storm passes tonight. We have a shortage of operators right now because they're out here quitting on me! I cannot afford to lose any more men by continuing in this awful weather. Do you hear me? Hey, are you alright in there?"

Denny was seated in the driver's seat. He slowly turned to look at the foreman, dead in his eyes.

"I think you may want to take some time off, too," added the foreman. "Did you come down with a cold? You're looking a little pale! You might think about drinking some cough syrup and get rest."

"There's nothing a good drink couldn't fix."

"Ain't that the truth," replied the foreman, who reflected on his grandpa's favorite and old medicine cabinet being that of the neighborhood bar. "Listen, I'm going to get out of this rain. I just thought that I should let you know about what's going on out here! If you have any issues with this, please contact the number on the back of my business card. Ask for Walter Snell in the morning!"

Without any emotion, Denny started his car and drove away.

By Ashaki Boelter

Chapter 3

Dead Meat

It was an odd night, as more than enough couples stayed home to woo one-another-half-seas over. The fierce storm turned the starlit night to clouded murky and reddened darkness, and its winds slowly flowed through doors, a melody of whistles and chimes for which death could dance. However, there were peaceful melodies of The Love Unlimited Orchestra on the company's music application that played through loudspeakers of Marshall Canny Corporation that calmed the nerves of David Snyder. He wiped away the final droppings of Mr. Brady's blood from the Human Resource office curtains; he spun his cloth, of a familiar ring, decades ago.

"That sure is one hell of a storm outside," he said to himself. The CEO watched the black car, full of mobsters, drive away from his company building with the corpse of Stephen Brady. "Besides me, who has ever seen those darkened and fiery clouds, which move like a foot race between a rabbit and tortoise? I warned that imbecile! And from up here, I can see that the entire city is covered in a twofold of darkness. In a matter of short time, we're all dead meat!"

David solemnly returned to his office and opened his mini-refrigerator. He reached in and grabbed a hidden bottle of whiskey.

"Lord, please do not strike this as my immense sin. With death around the corner, there is no better time than now to take a drink beyond my limit. Bless this whiskey as my healer."

With a glass of whiskey in his hand, David walked to and sat down at his desk. He threw down a large gulp of alcohol and sat still, without a rush. He had a home of strong faith, so he did not want to invite drunkenness into the presence of his wife and children.

"Oh, hell," whispered David as he poured another glass of whiskey. Again, he swallowed the drink. "What a freakish storm. I warned the fellow! The devil is upon us now."

A few more minutes passed, and the CEO poured another glass of whiskey; he contradicted his theory with healing time and an abundance of liquid courage. "This vampire thing has to be superstition. I do not understand why I am troubling myself over a tale that my looney grandfather once told me."

Lightning pounded the entire hellish sky and shook the Marshall Canny building to its core, but after David drank over half of the bottle of whiskey, he passed out in his office chair. It wasn't until an eerie shadow cast over his desk and a familiar, but uninvited voice grumbled that he came to light again.

"David Snyder, you should wake up!"

The CEO struggled to regain complete consciousness, but he opened his eyes and saw the last person he would have expected.

"Why didn't you make it clear to me about what I truly took from you, David Snyder? There was a dead body inside!"

David fully awakened from his drunkenness and sat up in his chair. "What? Denny, what are you doing back here?"

"You sold me a lemon! There was a dead body inside Woodland Yards, so I should sue you!"

"Denny, I certainly do not know what you're talking about with a body. I assure you."

"Who was in the urn, David?"

"Oh, you mean that ashes were found. I thought you meant that a full human body was found on the property. You baffled me there for a second. I know about the ashes if you should concern yourself. I'd rather not say who, but I might suggest you dig a deeper hole and bury it as close to hell as you can. Do not let the urn trouble you, do not open it, and for heaven's sake, do not disturb it."

"You play this game very well, David. You know who is buried in that lemon. I want you to say his name!"

Brilliance overcame David, as Denny's blank dark pupils drilled at his soul, and the corner of its mouth revealed a sinking fang. A drool slowly oozed from Denny's mouth and onto his chin. It became evident that Denny wasn't money hungry anymore, but rather the thirst for blood overwhelmed him.

"I will not entertain a promise I made many years ago never to mention that name again. And for all it matters, the lemon is yours. I will not pay you a dime because you stole it as-is, Denny. You do remember, yes?"

Denny replied, "You're right. It would not make sense to ask for my money back, which I never gave you."

"You're a genius, Denny. I knew that you'd come to your census, or rather their conscious by now. Now, if you don't excuse me, I have some rather important work to finish here. Show yourself out, that is, if you can remember your way around!"

"Before I leave," said Denny, "I've become thirsty."

"I could tell."

"Perhaps, David, you wouldn't mind showing me where I can find such sustenance."

"There's a water fountain down the hall."

David sat motionless, as a sudden drop of sweat slowly trickled down his face! It was then that he did not doubt that the tale was the truth of the vampire's resurrection if disturbed. Even if he wondered how it came to past, as merely ashes alone were not enough to bring back the walking evil, he sensed impending danger affront.

While the CEO slowly glanced at Denny's neck and discovered two deep gashes, which concluded that a menacing beast had bitten the former employee, he secretly reached for a gun in one hand. He readied his other hand to grab the crucifix under his shirt.

Denny shook his head in disapproval of David's water recommendation. "I shall require something thicker than water."

David quickly pulled his crucifix out of his shirt and stood from his desk. He pulled up his gun and aimed it at Denny!

"Get that cross away from me!" Denny violently crumpled against file cabinets, the walls, and then sprinted from the office. The holiness of the crucifix and David's faithful assurance in God's high power scared the malicious curse into a frenzy to hide.

David pursued Denny down the hallway! He fired gunshots at the fleeing ex-employee, while he held up the crucifix in his other hand. There was no place to run for the menace, as it approached the end of the hall. There, a window was placed for a scenic valley view of the city below. After the window shattered into salty crystals by David's bullets, the merciful vampire leaped for hell!

A mighty wind from the organic valley, rushed inside, as David nervously approached the glassless pane with his crucifix in hand. Had he defeated the vampire, he would have taken to rest and the bottle, but the breathtaking sight of the vampire's newfound ire compelled the CEO to now step back. There, of his utmost dismay, was a savior to the wretch's death sentence, the sinisterly Sir Sange. He carried his begotten follower in his arms, as he levitated away, with caution to the sight of the holy crucifix.

David's eyes grew wide as he stared in outright fear. His hands and legs trembled, for the stare of Sir Sange was mighty clear: Death was near.

"I remember you," warned the evil, dead soul. His voice was more in-depth with the baritone of a ship's horn. Sir Sange had eyes of rage, bloodshot in the reflection of a blood-quenching meal. He cradled his vampire spawning, who begged surrender to eat again on another night. "I will be back for you. Trust me. You will suffer for what you did to me decades ago! Oh, how you should consider yourself dead meat, David Snyder."

After hammering home his full intent of David's misfortunate end, Sir Sange and his new prodigy creepily morphed into vulture-faced bats. They hastily retreated away towards the plentiful forests of the Sylvan Hills because their new castle in downtown Portland was not complete.

David nervously pulled his cell phone from his pants pocket and called Lenuta, his daughter. He was wise to the situation, but not to the madness behind a vengeful scheme of Sir Sange. A warning was the least of his worries. The entire town of Portland was in danger, and his daughter was his first concern! However, he didn't call to warn or frighten her.

"Honey, I need you to call your aunt Johanna," said David, as he left a message on the voicemail. Unable to directly reach his sister because of torn family ties, he begged of his daughter's utmost attention to his word. "She has me blocked. Have her call me as soon as possible, please! It is of utmost importance."

Within minutes, his daughter named Lenuta begrudged to her poppa's frantic voice message. As far as she was concerned, she had more pressing matters at bay, on her overcast Saturday off from work, than her bossy dad's falling out with his viably decaying sister. At least between her poppa and aunt, they weren't far from forgiveness, but between Lenuta and her boyfriend, that was not the case.

"See, I allow you to get calls from men, and I don't complain!" The boyfriend, Curtis Styles, shouted and pointed with reason. "I heard the male voice on your phone. You don't see me going crazy!"

"That was my papa!" Lenuta was at the end of her rope. "I am not sure why you keep suggesting I may be cheating, but it certainly seems like you are either on your way to or you desire to. I cannot believe I caught you playing with yourself to an exercise video!"

"Is that a deal-breaker? Come on! At least I'm not out there sleeping around with different women!"

"You have me and don't need some exercise bimbo like her to get you off! Ewe! Curtis, you're a sex addict, and you need to seek counseling!"

"The only counseling I need is sex! Goodness sakes alive, Lenuta, you might as well become a nun, like your aunt!"

"Oh, you're going to go there, Curtis?"

"There's very little difference between your aunt, Sister Johanna Van Helsing, and you. You two beautiful women were blessed with beautiful bodies, but choose to let it rot away because you're both stubborn and stingy! For her, it's more divine and probably age, but for you, you're just stubborn!"

"So, you've got an itch for my old aunt too?" Lenuta glared over at the picture of her aunt on the hallway wall. "Curtis, please tell me you haven't imagined her and you."

"You're going to go there? Well, she is kind of hot!"

Lenuta had enough. "You're taking too long to leave, Curtis. I can call my papa back and have him get involved. He's a mighty businessman in this city! And you know that he wouldn't hesitate to fire you! Now, you get the hell out of here!"

Curtis took a deep breath and stood at the front door with a bag of clothes and a case of beer. "You know what, Lenuta? It is your fault. You should learn to take care of your man's needs more often!"

Slam!

Lenuta slammed and locked the front door.

"Lenuta!" screamed Curtis from outside the front door. "Come on! It's raining and strangely eerie out here! Can I at least have my hoodie? Baby, you're acting childish! Where am I going to go? I don't have a car! You're going to make me walk all the way home?"

"Hey, you black son-of-a-gun!" The next-door neighbor from a second-story window shouted. "Why don't you shut your trap so we can get some sleep around here, boy? It's the middle of the night! Why don't you make America great again and take that blasted ghetto behavior back to the other side of town with the rest of your thug Negroes! White lives matter in these parts, boy!"

"What?" Curtis scratched his head in sheer awe about the neighbor's critically and racially-charged comment. "Let me tell you something, you buck-toothed-having joke! Why don't you come down here and say that mess to my face, like a man?"

"Are you calling me out, you skinny little, black prick?"

"Come down here, and you're dead meat!"

"You wish!" The neighbor shouted back. "You're not worth the boggle, you nitwit. Why don't you run along to avoid being arrested! The girl dumped you, lad. If you had any smarts about it, you'd like high tail it to escape further humiliation! You can't force her to love you, idiot! Now, this is the last time that I am going to say this. You get the hell out of here before I call the police! And we all know that you don't want to deal with them!"

"Fuck you!"

"Go away, please, Curtis!" shouted Lenuta from behind her front door. "We are through!"

"Whatever!" Curtis surrendered and stumbled away in the odd rainstorm. "I cannot believe this, man! How could she do this to me?"

For miles, without bus fare even, Curtis angrily stomped through puddles and wiped raindrops from his face. The misty rain was so dense that he nearly needed to extend his hands afar for guidance to avoid walking into telephone posts or fire hydrants.

"She ain't giving me no' damn sex, so a man had to do what he done-did'!" Curtis reasoned with himself. "If Lenuta wasn't going to butter it, then there was no logical reason why I couldn't! Yeah, it's my ding-a-ling! I own the thing! I've been jiggling it since birth; that's natural! Yeah, it needs practice sometimes. That damn woman is trying to be a nun like her aunt and shit. Well, I don't need her!"

The stretch of road he traveled was bare and bleak, with cracking lighting from the sky illuminating only his flesh. Angrily, Curtis surrendered to the gusts and decided to rest out the drizzle under the shelter of a covered bus stop. The lonely young man figured that he had at least another two hours of walking time to reach home in the unexpected storm.

Indeed, his fears were unwarranted to unfavorable weather, and depression drizzled across his entire being, but a cold shrill suddenly climbed his spine as if the world were upside down. Sweat rolled up his back, for a feeling of danger was present.

Curtis stopped complaining about Lenuta's sex deprivation behavior and tonight's discovery because he heard something of a nearing hiss between the windy swish.

The young man cautiously looked right and saw nothing but the swinging light signal at the intersection. He turned left, and there was nothing. It was as if Curtis was the only person on the entire block that listened to the scissoring winds that pounded the fiberglass covering of the bus stop. Yet, the eerie feeling of being watched, or instead stalked, had overwhelmed him. Slowly, the young man turned all the way around on the bus stop bench.

There, Sir Sange hunched over as he stood on the other side of the bus stop's fiberglass shielding from the weather elements! Permanent shadows slithered upon his determined face with the ever-moving dark clouds and shifting lightning strikes he commanded. The vampire's raged eyes, of haunting hell's flames, and eagerness for blood-splattering gore, pierced through the fiberglass like a laser!

The ominous figure slowly opened his mouth and revealed his enormous fangs, drooled for a taste, and hissed like a hungry pet snake to an abusive owner that accidentally left the cage door wide open. The bus stop shielding had regrettably just three sides and was worthless from a diseased element, the cursed soul named Sir Sange.

"Ah!" Curtis jumped to his feet, spun around, and attempted to make a frenzied bolt, but he was quickly halted to a panicked freeze. The vampire came around to the front and blocked Curtis, who backed up towards the rear of the fiberglass bus stop wall. He was trapped, so he wildly swung his fists and kicked with his feet at the fiendish predator to protect his life.

Those defensive maneuvers were of no success, as Curtis' blood soon splattered against the fiberglass with dented force and drizzled down to the bench.

Curtis was more than dead raw meat. Sir Sange guzzled gobs of gutty and gooey blood from Curtis' neck. The dumped boyfriend began to seizure with green and yellow slobbery drooling from his lips, and his greyed pupils in his yellow eyes spilled into the back of his head. Curtis' clothes sifted to the ground, as many of his organs were slurped out through his neck. His body was depleted of all liquid.

The ruthless vampire slammed Curtis' bony corpse to the ground like a finished entrée of turkey bones at Thanksgiving, into a garbage can, after he satiated his thirst. The helpless victim's body was so drained; it camouflaged with the color of the covered, dry sidewalk under the wooded bench.

Sir Sange's thirst for blood was so high after nearly three decades that it was through mistaken delight and ecstasy with such a distinctive sweet deliquesce or only a suddenly forgotten cause for your use. Therefore, death or life was always a chance with the monster, based on taste or desired use.

After he satisfied his tumultuous thirst tonight, Sir Sange returned to the construction site to rest with satisfaction. The fierce storm disappeared into a view of stars and pale moonlight.

The distasteful melody of whistles and chimes, from which death's spurned assassin strutted, had softened to the human ears again. Miles away, nightmares of uncertainty swept through Marshall Canny Corporation; David Snyder had securely locked himself in his office and passed out over his desk. He had drunk four bottles of expensive alcohol because he knew that the bloody curse of humankind had resurrected; he understood that we were all dead meat.

Chapter 4

That was No Act

It was a morbid night, but as the sunlight drew nearer to the tops of Portland's highest buildings, one could have thought of nothing less than the city's beautiful and fresh landscape surrounded by roses. As the glistened mountaintops of snow and glittery clouds circled their waists, the radiant sunlight provided warmth across the smaller group of construction workers at Woodland Yards.

The freaky rainstorm last night not only reminisced of end-of-the-world revelation and rumors among construction workers but the added newscast that next morning, over the word of mouth, social media, radios, and television, caused a slight uneasiness everywhere.

From the homeless to business owners throughout Portland, many people caught wind of the gruesome news about a vicious attack at a bus stop last night. It was so cruel that many nearby businesses remained closed for safety.

There had never been such a morbid, animal attack. Perhaps it was a grizzly bear or a lion that bit into the young man's neck and depleted him of blood, the police detectives figured. They had never seen anything like that, and those who once held those jobs didn't call to warn. Instead, they called movers or simply got their families and bounced to the east coast.

Daylight beams of the Christian Sabbath crept through the office curtains of Marshall Canny and awoke David Snyder, who lifted his head from his desk and rejoiced. He slept through the terrifying night and now, wondered if such tyranny he discovered was just a nightmare.

David punched the keys on his computer keyboard to see if any news had reported anything wicked or odd since yesterday. There, on Portland's local media feed, was what he expected to find. He palmed his face and peaked at the article with absolute failure. Perhaps this was a direct result of the inability to have been wise not to have brought the vampire's body to the United States in the first place?

"But how could such a horrible creature become resurrected?" David thought.

Nearly thirty years back, the same plague came about in the City of Roses. As he recalled from their previous encounter, the withered corpse of Sir Sange was delivered from overseas to the science hospital upon Marquam Hill for study. He had such a reputation in England, Italy, to Romania, of unrealistic physical abilities for his size, unconventionally magical talents that used blood, and the mind of pure genius, those terrific fables were created of him similar to his notorious predecessor.

As history was told, his supposed birth name was Cecil Prendergast until he made entertainment headlines and borrowed the name Sir Sange. His new name, defined in Romania as blood, again gained a rapid reputation of a murderer, as his failing and incompetent magic birthed many deaths to his countless volunteers.

The law eventually arrested sir Sange during one of his late-night shows in Bucharest, where he would not reveal his true nature. There were many members of the Parliament in attendance, and he did not want to expose his evil truth just yet.

He magically escaped incarceration, so a countrywide witch hunt began. That is when the more and more local authorities took it on to find out who he indeed was upon his arrival. What they usually found was complete confusion. Not only had they found his claims of his birthright to be invalid, but Cecil Prendergast also did not exist on record anywhere. He claimed no ties to any family, any city, or any house. With as much fame he gained throughout that end of the continent, it surprised many that he had no trace. So, naturally, the authorities focused on a tale of a blood-sucking creature that the magician idolized.

A Sir Sange once lived in their Romanian land and also performed bloody magic many years ago. As it turns out, not only did people die in his performances, he accumulated a lot of gambling debt owed to prominent foreign and military leaders.

The original Sir Sange was captured, and the hired hands secretly executed him in a battle described as a War with the Damned. After the hired hand burned that conning magician's flesh, they covered up his death by separating and mailing his ashes in urns to many locations around the world. All of the countries, which he owed money to, received part of Sir Sange's ashes for complete repayment and satisfaction of his gambling debt.

For the locals of those Romanian towns and some military outfits in attendance of the original Sir Sange magic shows, they swore he was not far of imagination from magical and wicked resurrection. However, if he rose again after the separation of his ashes, they believed he would never be *whole* to stand up and vigorously fight for himself. At that time, that was the hypothesis of humankind, so everybody across the continent, most valid to the knowledge of the real villain, left his aging mystic parts buried in separate foreign tombs to be forgotten.

There was rumored an urn with some of the original Sir Sange's ashes buried in the United States but sworn to secrecy of its location by selective few who served in the military at the time in Romania.

Somewhat of a believed copycat artist than a genius magician, the tale and magic acts of Sir Sange overtook Cecil, nearly two decades later. He wanted to build a wealthier reputation on an obvious choice for widespread exposure to his show, so he also performed magic with using human blood. His naysayers, mainly the government officials and historians, who opposed his choice of bloody magic and name he took on, watched him become more and more like the real Sir Sange. Those who remembered him stayed far away.

His newfound magical fame brought celebrities, leaders, and new scientists to his shows. One day, it brought Johanna Van Helsing, of the notorious vampire-slaying family fable. She was a practicing missionary, who volunteered her own time in studying a long-forgotten cult of monsters on the side as a hobby. She grew interested in the rumored magician, as her family had once written of a similarly Sir Sange from years back.

Neither she nor her sister Daria, who inspired to move to America to attend a science university in Oregon soon, truly believed in the stories told in their family's diary. However, Sir Sange was on the level of Houdini, and his magic was printed as majestic and bloody. The two sisters figured the show was probably an adaption of the cult, which their family was akin.

It was Johanna that wanted to get a taste of their heirloom as she religiously studied the tales, but not the practice. Daria went for entertainment but had more interest in going to Amsterdam to watch the musical group, the Beatles, first.

Daria ran into David Snyder, an American tourist, at the Beatles concert. They found love during that concert in the john. She physically convinced him to also go to Bucharest to watch the phenomenal magician with her and her wealthy sister. He was proud to have had both sisters in his grasp but remained restrained from acting wild because of the many eyes of the paid and armed guards on the same bus.

Johanna and Daria were not widely known or recognized, but their family's fortune was great from bounty cases. It was Johanna that afforded that group of guards, as they rode the countryside towards more entertainment, without warning to the unregistered host and star of the magic show.

Once there, what Johanna witnessed in Sir Sange's magic show was the strategic perfection of a cruel thirst for blood. After she watched him drink a glass of "red wine" in front of the audience, she volunteered herself upon his magic act. Quite aware of the possibility that Cecil was somehow the same Sir Sange of her family's written tales, she also paid and prepared another group of guards at the event before his show. Should anything shift to hell's fire, the magician would be stopped.

However, something came over Sir Sange at his sight of Johanna Van Helsing. Boldly, he took her hand and assisted the beautiful woman to his magic wooded casket on the stage. Sir Sange could not resist the yearning of her brown eyes, the innocence of which he once had, and the beauty of her every pore. The magician was in love and lingered between a core of softness or hardness. An audience did not exist, for his five senses of taste were concentrated at a woman of brilliance, of style, grace, voluptuousness, flowery, and sculpting.

For the first time in his life, nothing mattered but the dark magic within himself, blinded by a fool's cherish of a woman's easiness by stature. There were no rings upon her finger, no companion with her, so Sir Sange laid her in the prop coffin and proposed a date.

"I would love to entertain you at my home if you should allow?" Sir Sange wanted her for eternity from the second he met her. He tried to stare into her eyes, tried to hypnotize her into an answer of his liking, but she comically looked away towards nearby guards. "You shall be my guest, woman! What is your name?"

"Go on," whispered Daria, who stood behind the stage curtain. She found Sir Sange to be quite handsome. "Tell the handsome man your name, sister. Lord knows that you need to get laid someday."

David was draped behind Daria and simply watched. He could not believe they had enough money to be seated on the same stage, behind the curtain. He attended the gory act with disgust. Everything Sir Sange did was bloody and life-threatening. David did not want any double dates with such a man and his newfound girlfriend.

"My name is Johanna," she hesitantly replied.

Quite past midnight, just as Sir Sange neared a sword through a wooded casket with her inside, Johanna slit her skin with a hidden razor. Before their arrival, she had privately briefed her highly paid guards on what to look for, should a real monster appear.

The prepared guards noticed the magician's gradual fangs appear! David was amazed by the magician's teeth trick!

"It is you," she whispered. Johanna shuffled in the wooden casket to free her weapon. "Let me properly introduce myself again. My name is Johanna Van Helsing, and you're in a lot of trouble."

Sir Sange loudly hissed with the failure of his cover. And of course, to the most notorious vampire slayer family, he was exposed as the only truth of the matter. The real Sir Sange had resurrected from the dead, and the name Cecil was simply a mortal cover!

"Look into my eyes!" The vampire hailed, as the crowd grew to the applause of his attempted role.

"No. I advise that you give yourself up to the authorities."

"Your act bewilders me," whispered the vampire. "Does your increasing heartbeat, the befallen blush upon your face, and the nectarous scent that trickles from body speak over your authority? Allow me to suck your blood, whereas you have eternity at your tips."

The class act opened his mouth to the sharpest fangs and leaned over to bite the life from Johanna, who appeared to gibber.

"That is cool!" David bought the act. "It's so real!"

"That is no act," said Daria. "He's going to kill my sister unless we get out there and stop him!"

Johanna suddenly shot her way out of the box with her pistol, as the guards wrestled with the so-called copycat magician! He shredded guardsmen heads off with his bare nails, bit others to death with his fangs, and threw guards into bloody gut splatter against walls!

David watched from behind the curtain in complete shock. There were bodies tossed everywhere, as was Johanna. Daria approached the evil vampire with her crucifix. She got too close, and Sir Sange slapped the necklace from her hand! She fell to her buttocks!

"You two are sisters?" Sir Sange recognized the matching beauty of the Van Helsing sisters. The guards and police officers backed away to find the best angle of attack, as the vampire circled Daria. "Nobody else will leave here a witness! However, two wives of my most notable enemy in Van Helsing is an improbable victory. Both of you would serve me as a wife, just fine. Your inescapable beauty eludes my intelligence of how the Van Helsing gene in women can be so attractive, but deadly."

"Leave her alone!" David shrugged his way through the guarded crowd, picked up Daria's crucifix, and held it towards Sir Sange's face! "You can die, you mother fucker! Go back to hell!"

As Sir Sange stumbled back into a wall of guards and police officers, in the retreat of the glaring crucifix, Johanna Van Helsing shoved everybody out the way and dove into the back of the vampire with a wooden stake!

That extremely sharp object pierced through Sir Sange's heart and out of his chest. That led to the vampire's death in front of the now scattered audience of guards and police officers.

The countryside wanted the decayed vampire body removed from the continent. Some of the people suggested putting the corpse on a rocket and sending it to the moon, but it was Daria Van Helsing that suggested she study his body for the sake of science at her school. Perhaps Daria would come across a lucrative discovery that would make Albert Einstein's, Maurice Hillman's, or the Wright Brothers' developments seem elementary.

The body of Sir Sange may have harbored cells that could finally combat common human illnesses and diseases. Johanna and Daria witnessed guards and police officers on that midnight using bullets and clubs on the vampire. Every wound healed up within seconds, and the vampire continued to fight without injury. It made sense at that time to bring the corpse to America for Daria.

David Snyder sat at his desk of Marshall Canny and further recollected life with his late wife Daria that became a student at a Portland science hospital. While she spent a lot of hours studying the vampire's wilted remains, Daria's new husband regressed into a lonely depression because she rarely came home to be a wife or a mother. It was Johanna, her sister from overseas that seemed to mother their daughter, Lenuta, by social media. Daria eventually hung up her scientific career, as she found her health failed. Indeed, in death, Sir Sange stole her soul without a bite.

Johanna also could not mentally overcome the deaths of those men at the magic show that midnight and took up the cloth to salvage her mind; she had also stabbed a man-figure to death that night. Armed with God's protection, Johanna tried to halt her sister's twenty-year, closed-door, research for fear that too much tampering with the vampire's body could accidentally bring forth the monster's resurgence. Johanna also realized that her sister's study of Sir Sange caused division at home.

The nun's niece, Lenuta, became a regular on the telephone and Internet with her, while Daria's husband sought leadership of his corporation and drank heavily during his daughter's teenage years.

Against her sister's will, Johanna poured money into a court order to end the research of Sir Sange and ordered the corpse to be cremated. That broke Daria's heart, especially since she got diagnosed with cancer and lost hope to cure even her disease.

With Daria's unfortunate and untimely death, David bought the Woodland Yards property for a tomb to stash all of her research. Nobody understood his resistance to ever build onto the shambled property. Nothing was thought out in entirety, but at some point, the property would have to be sold. Johanna's money was a significant reason the property remained with David.

Now, David's hand was forced. His ex-employee, Denny Brown, initiated the nightmare he always feared to come. He wasn't sure how Denny disturbed the vampire's rest. All he knew was that Sir Sange resurrected, remembered him, and would return to kill him. All David could figure now was that he needed his sister-in-law, Johanna Van Helsing!

He wanted to call Johanna, but he just couldn't erase the memory of his wife's last tears shed and final words of disappointment with her sister for not possibly finding a cure for cancer within the vampire's genes before she entered eternity.

There were times where the CEO thought it was possible to have somebody continue his late wife's research, but from what he experienced overseas upon capturing that beast, he promised himself to never let that thing out of its urn. Johanna refused to seek eyes upon it, as it was her sister's doing in the first place to bring it to the United States.

And, by chance, when David looked down at his cell phone, he read through a barrage of frantic text messages from his daughter. Throughout the swear-laden words, Lenuta repeatedly noted: A beast mauled my boyfriend last night. Please call me as soon as possible!

David called her cellular phone, but he got no answer. He texted her and did not receive a response. Concerned, David worried that his daughter might have also been attacked since he knew she and Curtis were in a growing relationship. So, David gathered up his keys and headed to her house.

Chapter 5

Bloody Vengeance

After David drove away from his daughter's suburban home, for she was not there, he drove straight to the church they usually attended on Sunday mornings. If such burdens existed, he was thankful to have rooted her to cast her worries on the Lord.

Just as David parked his luxury car and was about to get out, the radio deejay referred to the unfortunate death of a young local Portland man and asked for prayers for that family. The deejay identified the slaughtered man as Curtis Styles.

Last week, the very same Curtis asked David's permission to propose marriage to his daughter, Lenuta. Even though her father angrily said no, with time and maturity, David would have possibly agreed later. Curtis Styles was not ready for marriage, but he certainly had potential, more so than the other dogs she dated.

"Lord, have mercy on his dear soul," whispered David. He hastily stepped out of his ride, slammed the door behind, and entered the church. Once inside the sanctuary, he saw his daughter crowded about by Tongues-shouting church saints at the altar. The pastor of the church shouted for safety and peace for all of God's people.

Lenuta was a withered and broken mess, as she bounced on her two feet, fell to her knees, and shouted her head off to the Lord. She blamed herself for his death and cried out for forgiveness.

After the service ended, David joined his daughter in the church lobby. He protected his daughter from the news-press that approached Lenuta as she walked to her car. They wanted any information that she could share about the savage mutilation of Curtis Styles.

A few minutes later and back at the front door of her house, Lenuta and her father were greeted by the married neighbors.

"We're sorry for your loss," said the neighbor. He extended a box to Lenuta that was filled with a full course roast beef meal and a sorrowful card. He then looked at his wife, shared alligator tears with her, and sniffled as if he was calling out of work. "If it were the fellow we've seen here a few times, we'd like you to know that we are truly sorry about what happened to him. He seemed like a good fellow."

His wife added, "He seemed like one of the good ones."

"Okay, alright, thank you," said David. He nudged his daughter to unlock the door.

"Thank you," said Lenuta, as she turned the door handle and was bumped into her house by her dad.

Both of them sat down around the living room table. There was an awkward air upon David, accompanied by the silence.

"I asked him to leave," said Lenuta. "I dumped him last night, and maybe I should have talked it through."

"Are you blaming yourself for this?"

"I told him to leave. I did not even give him the hoodie he wore over here. I knew it was raining and still made him leave like that. He didn't have a car, and at that time of night, the bus schedule is not constant. What have I done?"

"You haven't done anything wrong," said David. "He and I may not have seen eye to eye on many issues, but I have to commend you for knowing what's right for you. Nobody in a relationship should stick around if they don't want to be with one another. You've shared weeks of concerns with me when it came to him. Nobody likes what happened to him. Speaking of, did you reach your aunt?"

"No. I guess that it was the furthest thing from my mind."

"You need to call her for me."

"What is it with you, not just calling Aunt Johanna yourself?"

"I cannot call. I won't call!"

"You sound like a bitter old man! That's my aunt, dad!"

"Do you want to know why I won't call her?"

"Go on."

"Your mother and I had a falling out with your aunt became a nun," said David. "It was around the time your mother found that she was slowly dying of cancer. Your poor mother wanted to continue her important lab research, but your controlling, rich, holier-than-thou aunt paid for a court order to stop her scientific stem cell research. Your aunt could not watch your mother work in such a fragile state. Even my money was not enough to keep your mother in business. Your aunt and her attorneys fought hard to shut your mother down."

"So, my aunt cared about mom and recognized it was best for mom to stop working. Why would you hate aunt over that? She cared for her sister's well-being."

. "I'll tell you," said David. "Your aunt broke your mother's heart. Your mother left this world with a frown, right in my arms. She said that she was close to finding a cure for her cancer. I held her closer to my face, and she whispered that her sister did that to her. Then, your mother was gone."

"That would be brutal for anyone to take, but that still does not warrant your avoiding behavior for so long, dad."

"Your aunt burned all of your mother's hard work from that lab. I could have sold the information, at least! Who knows what technology over the years would've done with her finding? Maybe somebody could've continued her work and saved lives."

"I thought you stored much of her work in Woodland Yards, dad. Why couldn't you simply place her most coveted research and work inside for somebody else to complete later?"

"Your aunt wanted it deleted immediately, and she had the money to carry that out. I could not stop her."

"Why would my aunt want to burn mom's work if it meant so much to the world? I do not understand. It doesn't add up. But I can now see why you don't want to call her. I'll reach out to her soon. I don't even know if the number is any good on my phone, but that's where using the Internet and social sites to find people is great."

"And I pray to God that the bodies around Portland do not continue to add up in the meantime," thought David. He walked away to grab a bottle of water, although he heartily wished it was a bottle of strong liquor.

"Dear God forgive me this Sunday afternoon," said Lenuta as she watched her father take a swig, "but I need a drink."

"Agreed," added her father.

"I think there's a bottle of gin and some fruit juice in the kitchen." Lenuta walked to her bedroom to change out of her church clothing, for sweats and tennis. "Since my girls are taking me out tonight for drinks at the Copper Penny, I'll have plenty."

"After what happened with Styles, are you going to chance going out there in the middle of the night? That is not wise! I forbid you leaving this house, young lady."

"Dad," said Lenuta, "you don't need to worry. Besides, not only are these ten of my closest homies, they all have military boyfriends that will join us. See, I will be completely safe. Trust me, dad, I really could use my friends' support in a time like this."

"Do any of these friends know the Lord?"

"Really dad, you sound like I'm that little girl that used to bring rotten dates home. I'm a woman now; this is my home and my life. And to answer your question, just so you don't continue to ride my ass about it, they go to church."

"That doesn't mean that they know the Lord."

"Well, they go to church every other week, so that should mean something. Now, stop worrying because I need comfort, not an interrogation. You know what dad, I'd like to rest. I do plan to have a late-night tonight. Maybe we can get together tomorrow. After all, it is a holiday, so perhaps we can do a barbeque?"

David moped in imprisoned silence out the front door. "Sure, honey, I like the sounds of that. Let's have a barbeque at my place tomorrow. Have a swell time tonight, and be safe. And please, don't forget to call your aunt for me."

David drove his car down the block, as he concerned himself into a stiff fear. He knew it was wise to keep an eye out tonight, for his recent glance and tone from the resurrected Sir Sange was of promissory vengefulness against him. It was fate that rewrote his chance of survival by Curtis' relationship with his daughter. He would not have known of the vampire's existence had that crossing at Marshall Canny never happened. Fortunately, he did know, and as he once believed, no vampires existed, so did the citizens of Portland, Oregon, not believe in such a bloodthirsty creature.

To tell his daughter of a stalking vampire in a time like that, while her mutilated ex-boyfriend was dumped and folded like sauced spaghetti in some morgue drawer, was a damned silence he had to observe.

David drove on down the street, suddenly marveled about the ridiculous speed that the new stadium was being built over his once-owned Woodland Yards. He shook his head with a disgusted grievance and took another glance while he passed.

A cold chill quickly shot down his back of the very thought that Sir Sange rested until nightfall inside the basement of that building.

David wanted to pull over and beg the construction workers to cease, but that could only infuriate Denny Brown. As time told, that bully had gangster ties and could put a hit on David. That would not have served any purpose not only to have gotten beat up but also, by chance, arrested. Then again, David suddenly thought maybe the cops would listen to him about what he suspected of a vampire.

"Yeah, right," thought David. He chuckled at such a comedic waste of time. He simply drove by the site and pondered thoughts of creating weapons to protect his daughter and himself.

Timely unaware, as such were the inhabitants of Portland, for that matter, the prior Woodland Yards property was indeed advanced into a rapid rise of mortar and bricks. The construction crew progressed quickly with the build of Denny Brown's coliseum. There were over fifty crew members that built above the reestablished basement, where Sir Sange rested in a coffin that Mr. Brown provided.

"Has anyone seen Denny Brown today?" The construction foreman stomped around massive lumber and concrete blocks. "I have Walter Snell on the line. He's been trying to reach his ass all day!"

A young construction worker approached. "I believe he's in the basement looking for something. I thought I heard his crappy cell phone ring down there a few times."

"Why won't he answer my calls?"

"Do you want me to run down there and get him?"

"No. I'll go. You keep an eye on the guys."

The foreman stepped over beams and opened a hatch to the basement. He entered and walked down the stairs into the dark passage. There, he turned on a flashlight to see where he was headed. The air was stiff, thick, and cold.

"Mr. Brown, are you down here?" The foreman pulled out his cell phone and dialed. He heard Mr. Brown's cellphone chime, but there was no movement. The foreman stopped and looked around. It was odd that with all of the demolition above, the beams and contents sat orderly. Unlike earlier, when his crew looked around the basement, he noticed brand new nails and screws in the supports, as if somebody had worked to keep the basement up.

There was never instruction to any of his crew to fix anything down there. It was going to be locked up until Denny Brown completely went through everything. It was dark down there, but small and freshly lit candles sat upon a few boxes.

"Mr. Brown, are you okay down here? Hey, I have my boss, Walter, trying to reach you about a cost issue. Because we're constantly replacing employees, dealing with worker's compensation, and speeding up construction production, we're losing money. Walter may want to pull out of this if you don't work this out!"

There was no response.

"Mr. Brown, this shit is creepy," said the foreman. "I don't know if you got a lady down here or if you're hiding or whatever, playing games, but I'm leaving you be. And I sure as hell don't want to run into a dead body; Lord knows you didn't look healthy earlier this morning. I'm going back up there now! To hell with this, dude, your spooky ass can deal with Walter Snell on your dime."

"Perhaps, that is for the best." That unfamiliar voice was so sinisterly deep and close that it seemingly came from the foreman's own lurking shadow.

Yet, as the foreman quickly turned and looked for the source of that answer, there was nobody there. He dashed back to the rickety staircase and stumbled his way up to the hatch door, unbeknownst of the hidden, reddened eyes of Sir Sange that watched him from underneath.

"You look as if you'd seen a ghost down there," said a construction worker to the foreman. "Are you okay? Did you find Mr. Brown in the basement? We're working these men too hard. Do you know that I've had another five guys quit, and three newbies drop-in, this morning! What's the deal with this Denny Brown wanting things done so fast anyway?"

As the construction continued above, below in the basement, Denny Brown stood attentive to Sir Sange.

"You say this tiny device is a mobile telephone?" Sir Sange pulled Denny's cell phone up to his curious eyes. He had never seen anything like it. He listened to the melody of the ringing chime and thought such an annoyance. However, if this was how the mortals communicated throughout the world, there was usefulness.

Nonetheless, his memory fluttered between haunted visions of actuality and numerous nightmares. He began to weed out tortured memories of his demise, as his dreams faded, such as ghosts.

"What country is this?"

Denny replied, "You're in the United States. And this is Portland, Oregon, sir."

"Tell me. What year is it?"

"It is 2021."

"That it is," said Sir Sange, as he looked again at the cellphone with admiration. "It appears that this place has preserved my well-being. I have slept for such a time. And now, I can again practice my magic acts once you have finished my castle. I will once again be the greatest magician ever known to humanity!"

"All you want to do magic?" Denny sarcastically chuckled. "With such power that you have, why not dream bigger? Perhaps you'd like to rule the world?"

"You think that ruling the world is big?" The sinister vampire laughed. "Do you think that I am the only vampire on this planet? If we all thought that way, with the will of humankind, every mortal would firstly perish in war. Truly then, vampires would stand-alone, with nothing to eat, and we could all die of thirst. Secondly, since we're of the human persuasion, it would not be far-fetched to imagine that greedy vampires would probably carry out cannibalism if we were all about power."

"But, you are the most powerful, my leader."

"There is always somebody more powerful than the next," stated Sir Sange. "To rule the world is to live in fear of those even closest to you, who at the right moment could strike when least expected to take your place."

"You do not fear me, right master?" Denny's greed was implanted in his genetic make-up, his bloodline, and his being. Sir Sange smelled his blood from the beginning and knew someday his servant would have to be destroyed. For now, Denny was a tool.

Sir Sange leaped at Denny! The servant stumbled backward and hissed. "No, I am not in fear of you. Do you understand?"

"So, your purpose for living is simply magic? You have unlimited power, and you cannot think of anything more than magic?"

"I sometimes think about the love of a woman."

"My lord, love to a woman is a hindrance to success."

"I beg to differ," said Sir Sange. "Success is meaningless if you have nobody to share it with."

"They are a hindrance, sir," Denny disagreed. "Success, along with a few hot dames without a contract, now, that is significant. Don't marry because relationships are nothing but trouble!"

Sir Sange rolled his eyes. "After all of these years, it is still true that Americans continue to live so carelessly and sloppy. Thank you for the update. While we're on the subject of this so-called great country, perhaps you can tell me how I got to the United States in the first place."

"I guess the previous owner, David Snyder, would be better to answer that question. You met the old bastard at the building where you saved me. He had you buried down here."

"Thank you for indirectly directing me to my purpose," said Sir Sange. "My memory is still a bit blurry, but I remember David Snyder very well now. He was there at my untimely demise many years ago. Please, tell me, does he also have family in Portland, Oregon? He and his circle will pay for what they did to me. A bloody vengeance will mine! I'll rip out their hearts and suck them dry!"

"I love your style, master!"

"Where can I find David or his family members tonight?"

"I always do my homework before I rip off or take what I want from a millionaire," said Denny. "I know exactly where David lives, and also, I know his family and where they live too."

The day had drawn to misty nightfall, and the deflated construction workers retired for home. There was no rush hour traffic on that Sunday evening, as malls and plazas closed around six. Traveling home was as fast as a blink of an eye. The dampened streets of Portland were quiet and limited of inhabitants.

That is, until Lenuta and her friends exited the Interstate 205 highway, in several beat-banging cars, and rolled up Foster Boulevard to the famous dance club called the New Copper Penny.

After they arrived and had a few drinks, Lenuta and her friends took to the accessible dance floor and enjoyed themselves with the freshest groove. That dance joint was the only excitement open later than most businesses on Sunday evenings.

The club attracted not only younger people, but older folks that had the bug to cut a rug, play video poker or pool, wanted company, or simply have a few drinks, also attended.

"Can I buy you a drink?"

Lenuta, who watched her friends on the dancefloor from the bar, turned to the unfamiliar voice. She gently answered, "No."

Denny stepped closer to her as the music was loud, and he wanted her to hear him. "Do you come here often?"

"Excuse me, but you're too old for me. And I'm here to enjoy my friends, not get picked up on. Do you mind?"

The bartender snickered and walked to the other end of the bar to hand out more beverages to people.

Denny wanted to call her a bitch right then, but such vile profanity was not in good taste of his master's inheritance or witness. The servant wanted to drink all of the blood from Lenuta's body with violent vigilance! Unfortunately, he was on borrowed time and a plan of Sir Sange, so his thirst remained in the imprisonment of cheapened bar shots.

"I'm loaded with money," bragged Denny, "and I have a brand new truck outside. Would you care to take a spin with me?"

"Please, you sound like a script. Listen, old man, why don't you save face, turn your old ass completely around, and hobble yourself back to the convalescent home you escaped from."

"That was rude! Young lady, what's your boggle?"

"What's my boggle? Do you mean what's my problem?"

"That's all I'm asking. It appears you could use the company."

Suddenly, one of Lenuta's girlfriends approached. "What's going on over here? It looks like you're upset, girl."

Lenuta looked up at Charlotte. Then she pointed to Denny.

Charlotte chuckled. "This chunky old man is flirting with you? See, I told you, girl. That's why you need to come on the floor and dance with us if you want to avoid played out old gees, like this wreck, flirting with you. Put down the drink and shake it off!"

Denny stepped to Charlotte. "I'm not some played out, old gee! All I wanted was some conversation."

"He wanted me to know that he is rich and wanted to take me for a spin his truck," added Lenuta.

"Yeah, right," Charlotte spat. "With that busted suit and cape, the drool coming from your mouth, and the slick hair, anyone can tell you're trying to find some coochie. My friend said that she isn't interested, so run along, or hobble, or catch ride-share to the other end of the bar before I get my military boyfriend over here to do something about it."

"Ooh, I'm so scared." Denny was not impressed or afraid. He leaned towards the sympathy card, as he could tell something truly bothered Lenuta. Whatever he was up to, he knew he could use that to his advantage. "I just made an awful mistake meeting both of you. I didn't come down here to be insulted. Thanks for your time."

Charlotte encouraged Lenuta. "Come on and dance with us."

"Wait for a second," replied Lenuta. She felt awful about how they treated the older man, as he walked away like a sad, saggy-faced puppy. "I'm sorry, but I'm not usually like this. Listen, the truth of the matter is that I lost somebody close on Friday night. I just need a little time to myself, and be around people at the same time."

"You lost someone? It must have been somebody close?"

"I lost my boyfriend," answered Lenuta. She watched Charlotte smack her lips and return to the dance floor. "He was found mangled at a bus stop by some animal; he'd lost a lot of blood. I'm hearing that the investigators think it may have been a bear. Nobody knows what attacked him. And I feel so bad because if I had never asked him to leave, he'd still be here!"

Denny grabbed the seat next to her. With intrigue and disbelief, he recognized the coincidence in fate, connected to his master.

"It's kind of all, my fault." Lenuta wiped her tears. "He didn't have a car. I knew the buses weren't running that late, and I made him have to walk eighty blocks to get home that night."

"Dear God, you don't say." Denny waved the bartender to get her another drink. Then he watched her guzzle that down.

"I was a terrible girlfriend with no patience or understanding."

"Why'd you ask your boyfriend to leave, being that it was so late?" Denny sat closer. "I read about that tragic crime. They believed it happened late in the midnight hour."

"I dumped him and shouldn't talk about that."

"I see," replied Denny as he signaled for the bartender to get her another drink. "Wait. I read that you're also the daughter of the man that runs the Marshal Canny Corporation. I used to work for him, but I've retired. Hell, you should be buying me drinks, girl! By the way, my name is Denny."

The bartender smirked as he had seen and heard a lot of flirtation in the past by players. He had indeed counted Denny out earlier, but now, he figured that the milky-skinned player had a chance to get some booty. The girl hypnotically looked into his dreamy eyes.

Lenuta chuckled. Her dad indeed shared his fortune with her, and she thought well of him. Therefore, she felt that others did too, and any friends of his were a friend to her. She suddenly felt safe with Denny and extended her hand for greeting. "I'm sorry for being such an ass. My name is Lenuta. It's a pleasure to meet you! So, you used to work for my dad? How long did you work for him? What was it like working with him?"

"Listen," said Denny as he waved the bartender over to give her another drink, "if you want to get some fresh air and have a better time, I'd love to talk to you more about that and take you for a spin in my truck outside. Plus, I can barely hear you over the music, and I'd love to answer your questions! It seems as if the deejay turned up the volume, and the place is getting crowded!"

"It has gotten louder in here! What about my friends?"

"Don't worry about your friends; they're having such a great time. They won't even know you've left!"

"You're right! Where do you want to go, so I can text my friends where I'm at?"

"Perhaps we can stop at Mt. Tabor, and you know, since I'm also a pretty good mechanic, go and test the suspension."

"What? No!"

"You're not going to allow me to hit it?"

"Are you crazy? It has to be the drinks that made me want to tell you anything, you pervert!" Lenuta was prepared to walk away.

"What, did you expect to find in this club, a priest or a pastor in here? You get your ass back over here!"

"Take your greasy hands off of me!"

Suddenly, an extended hand palmed Denny's face and shoved him aside. Lenuta turned around and saw Denny stand from the floor and sprint, as his master had planned, into the men's restroom.

"You must be whipped," said the bartender to the ominous, dark figure that sported a cape. "Are you going to stare into her eyes like a pervert or ask her out to get an episode?"

"Silence," ordered the love-struck stranger. His seductive stare drilled Lenuta's cornea, pupil, and vitreous humor. He tempestuously tickled and fiddled every strand of her optic nerve like a bionic banjo player. That sent a constant surge of electricity to her mind and caused her to pleasurably pant and breathe spasmodically.

"Oh my goodness, thank you," Lenuta exhaled. Her vision became blurry, as the numerous drinks also began to take its toll. After sweating circles around her barstool, via the stranger's excitement, Lenuta grew weakened. She fainted into the heroic stranger's arms, and he quickly carried her out of the building.

Charlotte and friends attended the bar shortly after. She looked for Lenuta, but could not find her. Then she looked to the crowded dance floor and shared the same failure.

"Did you see where my friend went?" Charlotte confronted the bartender. "She's the one that was here all night, and some older man came upon her earlier. Do you know who I'm talking about?"

"Yes, I do."

"Well?"

"She flirted with the old guy named Denny for a minute and then, I don't know, she left with another older and taller tanned man who thought it was Halloween. He came in here with a cape on with some kind of old school, Theo shag! They left about ten minutes ago."

"I wish you'd have stopped her," said Charlotte. "You know that she had drunk plenty of drinks!"

"And so did you," argued the bartender. "You're the one who left her horny ass with a stranger at my bar. So, you don't go pointing fingers at me! I'm only trying to do my job around here!"

"Well, fuck you then! You're an awful bartender!"

"If you're so concerned for her, go look for her or call a cop! I have drinks to pour. Now, can I get you and your friends anything before I go to attend the people at the other end of the bar?"

Charlotte angrily led her friends out of the New Copper Penny and into the parking lot. They looked through car windows and hoped she wasn't being taken advantage of by players. To their avail, they found only empty parked cars. Unsuccessful, Charlotte and friends stood on the Foster Street sidewalk and looked both directions.

"Hey, you over there, stop!" Charlotte watched Denny casually walk out the front door of the New Copper Penny with another young woman, who drunkenly stumbled and vomited over the sidewalk. Charlotte and her friends could tell she was not Lenuta.

Denny ditched his newly catch, rather exquisite meal, and sprinted in the opposite direction of the parking lot! He ran around the corner as if he were running on hot coal.

Charlotte and her friends dashed after Denny, and when they slid around that very same corner, there was nobody there.

By Ashaki Boelter

Chapter 6

Blood Bath

Monday morning had arrived, a holiday across the country that presented early mall shopping, house-cleaning tasks, barbeque preparedness, sleeping in, or exercise for most households off from work. As was the case, David returned from a five-mile jog and sat a spell for tea, bagel, and yogurt for breakfast.

The distressed father pulled his cell phone from his armband and realized that his daughter did not check in with him yet. It was an early and bright morning for many, but David was overwhelmed.

He dialed his daughter's phone number and immediately got the answering machine. David did not leave a message. Then, he texted Lenuta and received no response after ten minutes. Perhaps she got wasted and was still asleep. Or maybe, and unfortunately, as her dad thought, Lenuta went home with another man and had the night of her life in bed. Her father knew that his daughter was a wreck since the murder of Curtis Styles.

David scrolled through his cellphone and came across Johanna Van Helsing's phone number. David honored his wife's bitterness against her sister for so long that he could not fathom ever talking to Johanna again! However, the stakes were much higher after he came face-to-face with Sir Sange, who remembered him.

Johanna was the only vampire slayer he'd ever come across in his life, as the rest of the Van Helsing family was distant since the sisters disapprovingly came to live in America. So, there was no other course, then to make a call to the sister-in-law.

With a simple push of the button on his cellphone, David awaited the similar voice of his late wife to answer. Unpleasantly, but to have been expected, an automatic message blared from the receiver that his number was blocked.

David scrolled down and looked at one other number, which was never of the importance of his family or friendship chain. There, listed on his phone, was Denny Brown's number, which he kept in case of finding accounting errors while traveling abroad on business. From the altercation a couple of nights ago, the idea was not far-fetched that Denny was with, and now of, Sir Sange. If the bloodthirsty vampire had Lenuta, Denny could, with reason, possibly answer David's call.

Just as David pushed a button on his phone, an incoming call raced through from Charlotte!

"Hello?"

"Mr. Snyder, we lost Lenuta!" Charlotte's frantic voice caused static and uncertainty of what she said. Choked up and teary, she mumbled her apology through the stuttering of consonants.

"Say what? What do you mean that you lost Lenuta? Who is this? Is this Charlotte?"

"Yes."

"Now, slow down and take a deep breath. What did you say?"

"Mr. Snyder, we were at the Penny last night, having a good time, when some guy walked out with her. We looked for her, but we couldn't find her. We've spent all night driving around and looking for her. I'm so sorry! Has she called you?"

"No, but can you describe the guy? Did you call the police?"

"We didn't call the cops because we're not sure she didn't leave on her desire. She just seemed messed up last night. I went away from her to dance for one song, and when I came back to the bar, she'd already left. I saw her talking with one guy, but she didn't leave with him. The bartender said he saw her willingly leave with somebody else!"

"I'll try to reach her."

"I've tried texting and calling her all morning, but I've gotten no response. That's not like Lenuta! She's in a bad place after losing Curtis, and she would have texted me something by now. I'm afraid that something awful has happened! All I know is that the guy's name she was talking to when I saw with her, his name was Denny. The bartender said that she left with some guy in a cape."

David opened his mouth, but no words exited. His kitchen's stuffy air shrunk around David's face, as he frightfully daydreamt of a gored gobbed and sprinkling bloodbath of his daughter's gutty neck being greedily gnawed to the spine and pulled apart by giant feline daggers of the sensationally starved and revered vampire's fangs.

"Mr. Snyder? Sir, what do we do?"

Not even the gratifying glow of sunlight compared to the insatiable thirst for his new find, which Sir Sange harnessed in his blackened, dried, and rotted heart. Where David Snyder felt the ends of his lips sunken towards the depths of hell, the inherited vampire elevated to heights on angels could climb.

"How could this be?"

Denny opened his eyes and arose from his coffin. He turned to see that his master sat over Lenuta, as he was hours earlier. Nervously, Denny inquired his master with simplistic questioning. "Master, why didn't we just kill her? What is so special about the young wench that she has kept you up after the break of dawn?"

"She is all but a wench," answered Sir Sange. "She has a striking resemblance to a once, madly-loved mortal. No, it cannot be. My blind love for such a gene has me going mad!"

"Master, you're past your bedtime," reminded Denny. "It is daylight, and we should be at rest until nightfall. That is why your mind deceives you. You've been staring at that piece for a few hours."

"I cannot remove my eyes from her."

"Master, you told me that you wanted to kill David's family for what he has done to you. Her beauty is common. You don't need her to carry out your plan! Let us rest, and later, perhaps feed on her."

"Silence, now!" Sir Sange hissed. "I could render immediate satisfaction, and subject David to everlasting misery by taking his daughter as my bride! I see a win-win in the matter for myself. Besides, my mission here is not a success unless I can share it with somebody. I've explained that to you before!"

"I know, but—!"

"What would serve the purpose of doing such credible things and sit back and stare at a great memory, all alone? When I was once a magician, I would win applaud. I'd return home to a wall of silence."

Denny celebrated. "Well, I'm your guy! We can celebrate victories from here on out, together! You won't be alone anymore. I love you, master!"

"Shut up and return to your coffin!" Sir Sange demanded. He did not want his servant's love or empty promises. The sinister master, well-versed and self-knighted as blood, tasted and smelled greedy deception of his servant's once-warmth heart, whose blood matched the genetic DNA of many swindlers, the stench of foulness and rot, well before he turned Denny into the undead. "And leave us be, for I need to confront the soul of this woman, that I cannot resist, and address its departure in time with your presence!"

Without argument, disobedience, or tongue, Denny turned around and returned to his coffin.

Sir Sange carried over another candle and set it beside the coffin that Lenuta laid in, as his lustful gesturing overshadowed his face under the flickering movements of the bitsy, fiery wick. He leaned over and grew closer to his resting, well-endowed catch.

Lenuta suddenly, with the spring of a mousetrap, opened her fixed eyes and immediately became overpowered with desire and intrigue of Sir Sange. She had no fear; she had no will. At his silent command, with his slowly curling forefinger, Lenuta sat up in the casket that Denny created through the midnight hours with the extra lumber, nails, and tools at the construction site above.

Sir Sange reached his hand behind Lenuta's head, found his way around her maze of extensions, sensuously caressed and stroked her oily skin, and slowly pulled her to his face. He leaned in further, passionately kissed her massively glossed lips, and sensed her familiarity from her neck to her thighs.

The vampire master climbed into the wooden casket to sleep alongside Lenuta. Tonight, he planned to bite the hell out of her and turn her into his wife. Together, they slept.

Yet, Lenuta's father, fully awakened, had another course of added events for the same day, which pronounced that before tonight, the vampire was going to have to be confronted. This morning, still, David begged Charlotte to accompany him with rescuing his daughter.

"You and your friends should meet me and my security in twenty minutes at Woodland Yards! If it's not who I think it is, then you'll be able to identify the guys."

"I'm speaking for the rest of that we need to get some rest, Mr. Snyder. I haven't slept all night! Can it wait until the evening? Maybe she'll wake up somewhere and realize that she hasn't checked in. Better yet, if we haven't heard anything later, we should contact the police! That makes a little more sense."

"Trust me," replied David. "From what you described of the characters, I have a keen feeling that this is rather a delicate situation in which selective bargaining is warranted right now instead of the use of a nervous law enforcement's hapless and, may I add, ineffective bullets. And you know that I am a very influential man in this city; after I get my hands on the fellows I believe are responsible for this, then maybe afterward we can involve the police."

"Perhaps we should file a missing police report now."

"Right now, Charlotte, we can file a missing person report, but there's no telling how long before police would even take to get a search warrant. We don't have time! We must go before nightfall, or it'll be too late. I'll compensate you and your friends too!"

"But, what if they have guns? I'm not getting involved in some gang foolishness. I have a degree in Sociology, and I'm working on my Master's! I cannot be out there acting like some fool!"

"You've always been a great communicator with people since I've known you from my daughter's elementary days. I could use some help negotiating. All we need to do is talk to these guys. I'll bring some of my security, you bring your friends, and I know we will all be safe. Come on, Charlotte. She's your best friend!"

"It sounds like you're hiding something, sir, as if she's captured in some kind of drug or sex ring. It just seems as though the authorities would be better to handle this."

"Okay," surrendered David, "I will call the police if things get out of hand. I just think that at this point, if she doesn't recognize you or me, she may not want to return home. You may know something I don't to trigger her to come back. Please, Charlotte, I cannot do this alone. I need you and your friends."

"Fine," replied Charlotte. "We'll see you in twenty minutes at Woodland Yards."

However, within five minutes, Walter Snell and a couple of his associates, Barney Holmes and Kendrick Bellamy, entered the gated off construction site above the vampire lair, stumbled through the incomplete structure, and inspected the worker's work. The entire construction crew was miraculously given the day off, considered how hard they worked to complete a year's project in two months.

"Incredible," stated Walter. "The men have put their efforts into this project. Luckily, we haven't had more injuries, as fast as they are building! Has anyone gotten ahold of Denny Brown yet? I know it is a holiday, but damn it, I cannot even reach him during work hours either. I thought maybe we'd catch him around here."

"I've tried several times as well to reach the guy," added Barney. He stepped over a bucket of paint. "I met the comrade, maybe once, and I can tell you that he's always on the move. We'll just have to go about our business of inspection without him today. He probably just forgot."

"He's a terrible businessman," stated Kendrick. "He's never on time, he's greedy, cocky, and he's somewhat of a bully. It's probably a good thing that he isn't here."

Walter laughed. "What? Do you owe him money or something? He's a gentle giant if you ask me. He gets the job done, even when he doesn't have a clue on how to conduct business. That's all that matters here. Let's be cautious about such rogue success."

"Hey, fellows, come take a look at this!" Kendrick yanked at the cellar door that would not open. "It appears to be locked from the inside. What do you make of this? Come, give me a hand."

"That is a bit odd." Walter gave the door a hard yank as well. Barney joined, and all three men were unsuccessful. "Maybe Walter is down there. I mean, somebody has to be down there to have locked the damn door. Let's go on and find something to pry this baby open."

Walter looked for something useful and durable to do the job but knew that was a waste of time. "I'm sure that we do not want to tear up the door, gentlemen, but I manufactured every piece of wood to equipment out here, except for that door to the cellar or basement. That door is not from my stock, and if I'm going to guarantee my work here contractually, the materials used out here should come from my stock or sources! That door has got to go."

"And I'm sure that's one of the original doors to the old Woodland Yards, telling by the mildew," said Barney. "We didn't hire our men to do a half job out here. They should have taken that old door and replaced it. Let's use the forklift over there."

"Good idea." Walter stepped into the forklift and started the engine. He had no regrets for taking his action, and he wasn't afraid to confront Denny if he had a problem with the response.

Walter plowed the into the angled basement door and lifted the door off the hinges as if a feather.

The three inspectors looked down into the dark hall.

"Walter? Are you down there?" Barney asked. "Hello?"

Walter added. "You'd better not have this door locked because you're hiding from me! You're behind on the last project in payments. You need to compensate for some of the injury claims about this place.

You haven't answered any of my damn calls for over a week. It's time to talk, Walter! Are you down here?"

Kendrick hollered, "Alright then, we're coming down!"

"Don't go down there!" A distant voice shouted. It was David Snyder, who jumped from his parked automobile and stumbled to the three men with his cane. He stood between the door and the three inspectors. "Thank God that I caught you guys. Trust me when I say that you don't want to go down there."

"David, it's always good to see you," greeted Walter. He had done significant business with Marshall Canny Corporation for years. "But why are you here and with your security and those young people? What do you mean that we don't want to go down there? Your old boy, Dennis, doesn't seem to know how to conduct business, and after I get through with him, he may come looking for his job back."

"Well, I certainly would not hire him back."

"And I don't blame you," chuckled Walter. "Now, I don't know what you and your friends, carrying baseball bats, mean by harassing us by standing in our way to prevent us from inspecting this here basement, but that's bad form. Now, you get on' out the way."

Walter, followed by Kendrick and Barney, entered the dark stairwell. David led his two armed security officers and Charlotte's boyfriend and another couple down the staircase as well.

"I wonder why he suggested we bring these wooden bats." Charlotte's boyfriend whispered to her. "Look at mines! It's got baseball great Steve Garvey's signature on it."

Charlotte whispered back, "Mr. Snyder said it'll help with negotiation. We just have to look badass; we're not going to have to use them. Trust me when I say that Mr. Snyder is a good man. He would never lead us into a merry chase."

"I know," whispered the boyfriend, "but this feels wrong."

Walter was not impressed by the cave-like tunnel, as he headed towards the lit entrance to a room. To have this accessible was a hazard, and it just did not make good sense to him.

"Allow me," said David, who knew his way down that hall since he owned the place before Denny stole it. David recognized that the dim light was the same room in the basement where he placed the urn of Sir Sange. He gulped, as he led the group towards that room.

Walter had the ugliest frown upon his face and shoved David behind him. "You're walking too slow, scared of your own pace. We've got a busy schedule and no time to bleed! Let's go."

Walter took the lead, as everybody had faces of rage.

"Denny Brown, are you down here?"

Denny stepped from a dim room and confronted the group.

"There he is!" Barney declared.

"Dear God, man, have you not slept in a minute?" Walter was disgusted with Denny's appearance. "Did you not hear us calling you? Did you not hear your cell phone ring or see my texts?"

"Of course, I did."

Walter angrily asked, "Then, why didn't you answer? I've been trying to reach you for days! What kind of behavior is this? Do you know how many calls I've had to screen about injuries and lawsuits from employees that have quit based on work conditions?"

David shoved Walter aside, to Walter's and his two goons' disapproval. He frustratingly asked, "Where is my daughter, you sack of shit? I have witnesses that say you and your caped friend took her!"

Walter interrupted and gently patted his hand on David's chest. "Listen, David. We've got other business to attend to here than to ask about caped crusaders and superheroes or heroines having episodes with your daughter. Isn't your daughter, Lenuta, like thirty years old or so? Is she your childish trouble? Let the girl grow up! She's already burying the weasel by now. And your wife, bless her soul, died many years ago. We all have to move on, parent. And no offense, my friend, but we've got bigger fish to fry here! Thank you."

David showed just how old he was and socked Walter in the face. Walter flew into a mushroom cloud of dust against the cave wall. His nose exploded into a burst of bloody snot upon impact with David's knuckles.

"We're going to sue you for everything you got!" Barney screamed at David. "You can't knock Walter the hell out like that!"

Kendrick saw that Walter was out cold, but turned to continue their business. "Now listen here, Denny Brown! We don't know what you're up to down here, hiding, because that's how I see it, but Walter and the rest of us, need for you to come to the office. You're a very shady man to me, to begin with, and we need some answers to how you've been training and operating this crew with our tools and products. There are a lot of lawsuits on the table!"

"What in the hell is wrong with your teeth, man?" Barney asked Denny. He was stunned by the newly sharp fangs of Denny, caused by the delicious smell of Walter's blood.

"Denny Brown is going nowhere unless I tell him to go," answered a deep voice behind everybody. "The same goes for you all. This place is my kingdom for which you all have trespassed."

David, his two underpaid security officers, Charlotte, her hungover friends, and Walter's constituents slowly turned around.

David reluctantly whispered, "Sir Sange, the bloody curse of humankind is alive."

"And your lives are now a mere smidge of ink upon your family tree," said Sir Sange. He stood in the lightest of shadows, as mostly his fangs could be seen whenever he spoke. A fiery red lining outlined his angry, bloodshed eyeballs and pierced darkness, fixed directly upon David Snyder. He growled and added, "Some of you, my servant, and I will violently feast on you alive. Only one of you will remain unharmed; I have a certain plan for that one."

"What did you do with my daughter?" David hollered at Sir Sange. "Where is she? Did you kill her?"

"Ah!" Kendrick screamed as Denny's lips curled over the inspector's neck. Alarmed, he tried to fight off the savage vampire, but even his hatred of Denny did not drive enough adrenaline for his necessary willpower.

Denny demoralizingly sucked and willfully guzzled down Kendrick's thin blood, as if his victim's neck was a plastic straw of jammed frozen strawberries until air bubbles could be heard boiling at the bottom of Kendrick's stiffened toes. Then the vampire's servant glared at the rest of the terrified group and angrily ripped a mouthful of a gutty esophagus and torn skin from Kendrick's now dropped body.

"No! No! No!" Charlotte's boyfriend suddenly belted a scream of helpless despair, as his entire head was palmed within a pimply claw of Sir Sange. The boyfriend held onto his girlfriend's hand as long as he could, but his heavy perspiration caused him to slip into the full grasp of the master! Without any chance to defend, the young man was digested into lurking terror behind the master's black cape; sliming blood dropped onto the dirty floor between the scrambling sneakers of the drained victim. The thirsty host of terror munched, gnawed, and sucked his rattled, jolted, and shaken victim dry and dropped him to the dirty ground like a sack of chitterlings.

"Oh, God, no!" cried Charlotte.

"Gustos!" Sir Sange stupendously declared. He powerfully stomped on one of the boyfriend's eviscerated eyeballs and wiped its mucusy secretion under his shoe across the muddy ground. Then he looked up at Charlotte and stated, "You have good taste in men."

Charlotte backed up as she cried and slobbered with utmost fear and underlying defeat. She had not signed up for any of this!

Sir Sange licked his chops and opened his arms wide. He joyously smiled to welcome his next taste test. Blood drizzled down the corners of his mouth, as it was also now marveled that his pale face had morphed into a creature, not of this earthly realm.

With patient hunger, the vampire's ears pointed up like an alert wolf and his eyebrows expanded to a patch of a hair, bushier than a near handful of tobacco. Eerily, smoke floated from beneath him, while his eyeballs turned entirely black from bottom to top. The master vampire's eyelids were stained with reddened rash and extended webs of green and blue varicose veins. He seemed undefeatable, strength unmatched of even one-hundred men, as he trapped everybody from escape. Sir Sange hissed like the earliest garden's serpent, desired to once-again, in liking thereof, to kill all of humanity.

One by one, both master and servant strong-armed the helpless inhabitants of the cellar with the feeding frenzy of starved sharks within the ocean of a prehistoric apocalypse. The fearfully panicked mortals tried to defend themselves with the wooden bats they brought brainlessly, but the vampires skillfully dodged and overpowered such production.

Bones cracked at the crushing pressure of fangs, flesh pierced and tore by extended vampire nails, and blood worshipped of taste. Sir Sange and Denny savagely mowed over nearly everyone in the dimmed hallway. A bloodbath was an understatement until a blare of light suddenly cast upon the back of Sir Sange! It came from the cellular door, which was opened wide.

Sir Sange stopped his massacre with a handful of Charlotte's blouse in his arm and retreated into the shadow of the tunnel wall. Denny continued to hold David in a full-nelson.

Down those wooded steps, two worn loafers slowly revealed, but nothing of fancy. A holy woman approached, who was a serenity of motherly hope. It was Johanna Van Helsing.

"It is you," welcomed the gracious vampire, for he had many dreams of such beauty during the last thirty or so years of his capture. "How can this be? How could whom I have captured, be your twin?"

Johanna took a step towards Sir Sange. "And you are just as mystifying and beautiful a creature as many years ago. To simply answer you, my last of covet, my sister married the man you seek to kill there. You have his daughter, my niece."

Sir Sange was amused. "Fate has been too kind. And the Van Helsing bloodline is so addicting. Well, I don't want a grandmother version of such a desire, as you are neither mystifying nor beautiful this age. I'll stick to the young and tender Van Helsing I choose to marry tonight under the full moon. So, I believe that you're going to have to be the one who diminishes."

"I'm afraid that her father and I disagree with your proposal to marry Lenuta," stated Johanna. She bravely held up a very shiny crucifix to Sir Sange and also, Denny! It was a light of hope, with no darkened borders, as bright as our Creator's first.

Painfully agitated and overly ashamed, and with disorderly retreat, Sir Sange and Denny dropped their assailants to hide. Their own two feet were not quick enough to escape the fiery end that awaited their rogue souls at the image and reminder of God's begotten son with whom they also rejected. Their bodies began to burn, as they scrambled for relief and finally reached their coffins.

Johanna followed the evil monsters into their candlelit lair and watched them hastily close themselves in their coffins.

Charlotte ran for her life and climbed out of that basement. She screamed at the top of her lungs, but nobody heard her on the holiday morning.

David picked up the wooden bat that had been knocked from his hand and snapped it across his knee. He held it up and admired the sharp break of that bat, which now had a pointed end. As Johanna, he also was versed in vampires since he first adopted sight of Sir Sange.

Next to Johanna were three coffins. David quickly opened the one in which the two vampires did not climb. There, he found his daughter Lenuta, breathing, but as if she were in a coma with her eyes wide open! He called her name, as her eyes followed his finger, but she did not respond with bodily movement or voice.

David did not reach for her, in fear that she may have been changed to a vampire, but he noticed no bites on her body.

Johanna warned him. "David, there is still a chance at saving her."

"What did he do to my daughter?" David grew with concern and rage. He stumbled away and flung the door off of the casket in which Sir Sange rested!

Without a tremble of fear and a sinister stare at David, for he would not rise under the guidance of the parishioner's faith and her overbearing crucifix, Sir Sange remained a villain willfully imprisoned.

"What did you do to my daughter?" David held the wooden bat above his head, readied to stab the vampire. Sweat trickled down his forehead as his risen hand began to shake. "Release her!"

"I will not," replied Sir Sange. "She will be my wife."

"I don't approve, you bastard!" David could not hold his patient instinct to kill any longer! He dropped his fist towards the head of the solemn vampire, hoping to drive the wooded weapon through and into an explosion of brains and guts. Instead, to David's bewilderment, Sir Sange expeditiously tilted his head away from the impact of the sharp end and watched his adversary stab the pillow.

Johanna stood prepared, but Sir Sange knew not to lunge from his resting place. Weapons formed against him were of the greater good, and he had no chance for or in hell. The only thing the master of darkness hoped was relevant to his survival, at possibly his last hour this time, was his godly defiance to believe the almighty creator made a mistake by developing a heart of humankind the ability to forgive.

"This is the not the time or the way," whispered Johanna.

"What are you talking about?" David lifted his wooded weapon from the busted pillow in the casket. He stared back into the squinted eyes of Sir Sange.

"Put the door back on the coffin," ordered Johanna. Were the saint's wisdom and experience suddenly overclouded with love and divine forgiveness? Her decision to not end the vampires was divisive.

"We need to kill him right now!" David was reluctant, as his daughter laid in a trance in another coffin. He watched Sir Sange smirk, straighten his head, and then proudly close his eyes. "This creature made it a complete bloodbath down here! He needs to die, Johanna! Now is our chance!"

"I said for you to put the top on the casket!" Johanna demanded again. "Trust me, David. Was I wrong when I disagreed for my sister to bring that evil plague to America to study? I would have never come here, in the first place, if it weren't for my love and support of and her. This country had the advanced tools and science at that time, which she figured, could help her pursuit a cure for cancer. Yet, after many years with this spectacular creature, she could not find a cure, so I shut her down before she resurrected him."

"She wanted to resurrect this vampire?" David felt lied to, for he had not been told of that by his late wife. "Why did she hide that from me? That's an insane idea! Even when I read through her final journal entries, there was no writing of that."

Johanna watched Sir Sange confidently close his eyes to rest. She answered David. "Firstly, she did not want to be remembered historically as a lunatic, a truth for most Van Helsing members, especially those who have come in contact with vampires. Nobody believes they exist, but us. Van Helsing members are the crazy ones."

Sir Sange smirked.

Johanna continued. "Secondly, can you imagine her journals being found in the public domain, firstly of bringing a well-documented corpse back to life and letting everyone in on the reality of vampires' existence by how she raises him? Of course, she could not record those entrees. Imagine a world that knows vampires exist! Imagine the hunt. Imagine science. We saw what happened with witches back then, but can you imagine today what a vampire hunt looks like then? It would be hard to tell us apart, and so much innocent and guilty bloodshed would divide this place."

Had David been wrong about Johanna all that time, for she talked of truth and sense? All those years, he believed that an impatient Johanna wanted her sister Daria to stop the research and burn away the work. Her consensus was that her research was a dangerous waste of time, after so many years of research, and a foe that no Van Helsing would ever entertain to live past their forever warring confrontation.

However, David believed Daria was a different kind of Van Helsing, daring and willing to advance humankind's past illnesses using vampire biology instead of exterminating the creatures. Her heart was in the right place to help our civilization.

For all the years past, David believed Johanna just couldn't get over it, like the rest of their Van Helsing family, who eventually cut off both sisters for such a mockery as using a vampire for scientific exploratory on foreign soil.

"Allow me to help you with the lid," said Johanna.

Johanna cautiously helped David with the coffin lid and secured the casket. "David, I did not end her study to kill her. She was dying faster as she tried to find a cure; she had no peace. And to be frank, Sir Sange would have killed her before any cure to cancer was found. For heaven's sake, Daria was about to bring him to life!"

"She never told me that, Johanna."

"David, she told me that with Sir Sange being alive, it would show how specific systems worked in his body so that she could compare his system to a mortal body. That could give her more insight into how his body cures. You see, that kind of thinking is why I had to end her work. There was no way in hell I would allow her to bring him back to life, a chance to kill my sister!"

"I didn't know that."

"That's why I demanded this vampire's body to be cremated not to risk anyone else continuing her work, especially not having the experience or expertise that my family has with dealing on how to kill this monster."

"What do we plan to do with Sir Sange now?" David thought about the fate of his life, should they carry on with the vampire's survival. "Tomorrow, the city will be alive again. Today is the best time to get rid of this thing once and for all. There isn't a chance I'm willing to see this situation through the night. He will be too powerful!"

Johanna replied, "They never go away once and for all. Don't you understand, David? Vampires come back to us based on the lack of merits of humankind. If you think this place won't be dug up ever again on American soil, and his body found, ashes or whole, then you're not thinking clearly. Where, or more importantly, when will we find Sir Sange next?"

"I'm not thinking clearly? We've got him trapped and hold the weapons to end him right now! Once he's dead, his spell will fall away from my daughter. It will be a happy ending!"

"Sir Sange needs to be returned to his land," said Johanna. "I have already arranged a flight to carry this thing back."

"I don't like that one bit."

"The vampire will be arraigned in the judicial system for his crimes overseas. So be it, per the Van Helsing elders. I am no longer fit at my age to monitor his sleep in the United States. I, too, have cancer. I am dying. David, it is the right thing to do to protect us all."

"I'm sorry to hear that you're dying, but you're giving him a chance to escape by moving him! We can kill him right now!"

"You and I are not killers," answered Johanna, who was allowed to lock the solid mahogany coffin of Sir Sange. Denny had served his master well, finding such a fitting and comfortable design. "We'll let the law handle him."

David was shocked. "What? The law makes mistakes too!"

"The law is corrupt in the United States," interrupted Johanna, "agreed, but it is for sure that justice would not know how to handle this kind of evil once he revealed himself. Overseas, we know this vampire. Let God do his bidding, to rest the souls of those who were condemned to an untimely death. I am only the messenger, and I live by His instruction."

"Sir Sange is playing you all like a fiddle! He's so smart!"

"Vampires are very smart, you're right." Johanna cleared her throat. "For instance, this vampire once fooled people to believe he was Cecil Prendergast, a local magician. My family found the remains of that failed celebrity deeply buried in the foot of the Carpathian Mountains. We know who Sir Sange is and his origin. He was bitten by a very famous vampire in our parts, mostly written about in my family's diary. "

"What about my daughter?"

Suddenly, Lenuta quickly sat up in her coffin. She wiped her eyes, and frantically looked around. "Daddy, where am I? What's going on? Is that Aunt Johanna? So, you got my text messages!"

"I did. I came as soon as I could." She studied her niece.

"Can somebody give me the correct number?" David asked. "The number I got for you, Johanna, is disconnected."

"Daddy," Lenuta chuckled, "you two need to work things out."

"Lenuta, darling, is it you?" Johanna turned, hopped over to her niece and held her crucifix at her face. There was no surrendering reaction. The spell of Sir Sange was lifted from Lenuta. "It is you!

Sir Sange has released her, for it is the wise thing to do. I told you they could be reasonable and smart creatures."

As Lenuta hugged her frail aunt, Denny quietly and slowly sat up from his coffin. The dangerous crucifix, as he saw, was well-buried within the DD bosoms of the embraced aunt and niece.

Lenuta's father awaited his loving moment for gratitude, but he regrettably heard the distant crack that came from Denny's spinal arthritis. "What in the hell; you've got to go!"

Denny hissed for his recognition by David, but he was commanded to focus elsewhere. The servant fixed his sight on Lenuta, as he slowly opened his mouth, full of drooling fangs, and prepared to leap out of his casket to kill!

David raised his wooden weapon, dove onto Denny, and repeatedly struck the vampire servant through its black heart until it pureed and poured out of his back from many holes like strained pasta.

Sizzling, dark blood splattered over all the coffins, all over the walls, and all over the startled mortals. It was a slaughter described as a diplomatic absence of moral compass for many reasons, on the top being the unbalanced justice system's current grasp of Denny's continued killing and criminal behavior. By instinct, David took the law into his own hands to protect his daughter from the beast of the servant. He wondered who was smarter now.

For Sir Sange, it was a painful reality that he seemingly was on the shorter end of the stick for any resemblance of a happy ending. However, he had anticipated that Johanna came to bring him to justice, instead of death, the moment she and her religious clergy stepped upon the property. He learned that the United States was a strong and mighty country, so he hadn't come up with a foolproof plan of how to rule. Yet, the power it had was also its corruptness and virus.

Sir Sange saw Americans as scarily complicated and uncalculated from the rest of the world. The country thrived in love and hate. There was no winning side to any of it, repeated discrimination, loving speeches, voter fraud, celebrated marriages, police brutality, medals of Honor, murder, adoption, love, baptism, or childbirth. Everything was a clashing battle, a war, and a constant game of wins and losses to a melting pot of love and hate. The country was headed to self-destruction, which caused a lack of interest in Sange. For him, it seemed as if he would inherit a lemon.

Now that Johanna showed up, his plans changed. For it was the gibberish, he remembered, at his demise of her hands over thirty years ago that thwarted his renewed idea. Unlike the other Van Helsing family members, he knew that Johanna would not allow his death, like before. She did not kill him then, and nor would she today.

The vampire awaited her plight, her bargain, or plot. Sir Sange did not truly any court could genuinely harm him, so he allowed himself the patience of arrest, enthralled with the next adventure of Johanna's perhaps farce.

Along with the continued showing, several men and women, dressed in black robes with hoods, and paid for by Johanna, entered the basement. Directed by a local undertaker, those local and temporary employees picked up the casket of Sir Sange, for minimum wage, and carried him down the tunnel, up the stairs, and into the radiant sunlight for transport.

Chapter 7

The Bloody Curse of Humankind

Trails of uncertain exhaustion and gray lines of foggy relief gracefully lingered towards a fiery blood orange sunset, as a lonesome commuter plane with twelve cramped passengers, three pilots, and one monster aboard soared the endless and dismal atmosphere above the raged Atlantic Ocean. Flying towards the pale face of the splotched moon over England, inside, Johanna Van Helsing calmly walked away from the pilot's cockpit. She had informed the pilots to prepare for a bumpy ride and forewarned much more extreme turbulence, unbeknownst to the dashboard meters, was about to begin. As soon as she left the cockpit, they locked their door and cocked their gats.

Neither of the well-compensated pilots knew of whom or what they had locked in cargo, but they were just made aware of the dangerous capture's unmatched, escape talent. Riddled with such a seemly farce, the pilots turned their attention to talk about those magical movements of Johanna Van Helsing's inspired physique, and her steps of erectness, arrogance, and conceit, as she slowly exited the muggy cockpit.

"God made a mistake taking that old bag off the market," stated a pilot, as he listened to a nearing airport center controller. Then he flipped a switch above his head and responded into his mic, "Copy Heathrow, Central Elite 98, 340."

"Is she a nun?" One of the pilots wasn't sure. "Maybe she's only a Christian who dresses modestly in a long dress. I was about to ask her out! Nuns may be restricted to date, but there's nothing wrong with snapping up a wholesome Christian girl! But seriously, fellows, you know why we can't even go there with that sexy woman."

"Yeah, I mean, did you see the luggage out there? Good luck with that. Now, can we pay attention to flying?"

The pilots looked at each other and agreed just to fly the plane.

For her upward age, the aroused pilots had agreed that Sister Johanna, as many called her back at home, was divinely lucky to still look so naturally bouncy and loose in her wedged dress through all the violent turbulence. However, there was no chance that any of the three pilots would drop a line on her because of her luggage, the other eleven thugs she hired for protection to accompany her.

Brutally massive and healthy in muscle shirts, stubble across their faces, and frowns that would outcast a saddened mime, Johanna's bodyguards were nothing short of the most notorious gang members from Italy's and England's meanest and threatening syndicates.

"Are those pilots giving you a hard time?" Angelo Ricci, a plump and juicy thug with many swollen varicose veins on his forearms, grabbed Johanna's wrist. He stopped her. "I saw the way they stared at you when you left the cockpit. Do I need to talk to them, holy sister? I can fly this plane if I need to dismiss any of the pilots."

"No need for any of that. I'm sure the pilots were only struck with flattery."

Angelo Ricci finished wiping his machete into a shine and then picked a piece of chicken from between his teeth with it. He sucked blood from his slit gums, placed the knife into his holster, and let Johanna pass. "I know you're from a very profitable and famous family line. I do not question your faith-filled intelligence of merit or about what kind of boxed trophy lies below us. I'm only stating the obvious to us that this doesn't seem like a dangerous flight to warrant all the finest killers, church lady. Am I missing something?"

"Just be patient," said Johanna Van Helsing. "Trust me. There is satisfaction coming, guaranteed. Warm yourself up and get the blood flowing, boys. Keep yourselves attentive because once it escapes, and trust me that it shall, it could be a draining experience."

"Yeah, okay," chuckled a hired killer. "Whatever, you say."

All of the hired killers laughed at the idea that anything would defeat such a skilled group of professionals.

"Lady, trust me. Your life is in good hands with us."

With puckered lips, laughed at and dissed, Johanna returned to her seat and nestled next to a window. With the blank stare of a cautious cat into the dark starry night, she was not stargazing or praying, for that matter, but listened for odd noises outside of the standard plane mechanics.

The faithful, fraudulent woman knew that it was only a matter of time before Sir Sange would physically make his presence known to everyone aboard. The strayed madness to Johanna's logical attempt for justice was a mere diversion, while her honorable acceptance of her Godly faith gained public concession and dwindled into her past. She acted her clergy role with flying colors and drew up a mockery of religion to gain typical respect from her niece and David Snyder.

Johanna was nothing more than an old, retired, and front-row holiday-only churchgoer of a rugged church in northern California. Over time, as she spoiled most of her life in front of a television or a computer, she gained enough retirement and social security benefits to afford her bodyguards and plane expenses.

The faithful fake kept in touch with her family overseas, which also sent her money on occasion. In return, she relayed to them thanks and never bothered a word with them. In other words, they had no idea of her arrival.

After the death of her sister, Johanna began a spiral into her lack of faith. She became flawed to the degree that she feared death.

And after many symptoms of her life dwindle, and the recent hospital visits, never in her life would she had ever thought that a doctor would tell her that she had two months to live! Therefore, if her desperate gamble succeeded, that would be the end of her most notable foe called cancer. Johanna did not want to go through the misery that her sister went through.

Indeed, with a demising hope of eternal life, she rottenly believed that Sir Sange was her savior to live. Since he would have sensed true faith in God upon reflection of the crucifix of the beholder at that construction site, Johanna figured that he must have reasoned with and knew he was being spared the troubles becoming in Portland, Oregon.

Sir Sange had a chance to return home, to entertain a masterful art of bloody magic, and another opportunity to take Johanna as his lover! Together, that had something they wanted of each other, and it did not matter if the plane crashed into the depths of the ocean. If the plan worked, neither Sir Sange nor Johanna would have gone down with that plane.

The lights upon the plane began to flicker. There wasn't a hired killer aboard that was afraid of a little turbulent weather slapping against the flight. They were focused on the matter at hand.

"Aye, are you going to take all day in there or what?" One of the hired killers stood next to the bathroom door at the rear of the plane. He repeatedly banged on the shut door with his fists. "Come on. You've been in there for quite some time. I have to take a fucking dump, my friend! Do you hear me? I got to go bad!"

With the flickering dome lights inside the plane, one minute, the door was closed, and at the next flicker, the door was wide open.

"Holy shit, man, what the fuck?" The hired French killer pulled his pistol from his belted holster and was about to lift his and fire off a shot. He was overwhelmed with the strength of the old blocking hand with long fingernails that intercepted his gun upon the pelvis! "No-no-no, help me, comrades! Get him off of me! Ah! Gurgle…Oh shit! God, help me! Gurgle… Uh…" Blurt-slurp-slurp!

The tall, dark and ominous villain let go of the blood-drained corpse and loudly hissed at the armed passengers! Sir Sange stood unsatisfied with one death, as his victim's arteries and bloody gobs drooled from his razor-sharp fangs.

Everybody, but Johanna Van Helsing, stood from their chairs, with their weapons ready. She calmly stated, "Meglio se aiuti il tuo amico, Angelo."

"Now, this is what I've been waiting for!" Angelo stood along with his armed fellows. He yelled out, "Mangia merda!"

The hired-hand lifted their various guns and angrily fired rounds of multiple bullets directly into the vampire, who was unaffected! No direct shots sailed out of the once-fabled beasts among the living. The unmoved vampire absorbed every round as if they dissolved within his body!

Johanna Van Helsing turned to her window and mentally blocked every scream and tearing of limbs from her mind. What she ignored was the savage mutilation of every brave villain she could afford.

Johanna once flinched, with her shoulders high. Blood splattered from over her shoulder and landed upon the top of the seat in front of her. The selfishly negotiated woman had no desire to help gangsters, for she hired them as feeding for a thirsty lure to her plan.

Then, within seconds of the last single gunshot, there was ear-plugged silence from the withered chaos. Blood rolled down the only aisle with the aid of turbulence.

Sir Sange took a couple of steps and stood alongside the row where Johanna Van Helsing sat. He puckered his lips, turned to her, and sat beside her. There, he licked and rubbed human fragments from his sharp nails and popped his knuckles.

As she listened to the grimy, slurping, and slimy noises between the vampire's mouth and his cupped fingernails, Johanna was terrified of the disfigured and hairy-faced beast. She exhaustedly questioned her lack of morals, decency, and genius. Perhaps senility overcame her intelligence, as the very creature that her family despised and of their infamous lore was upon her for defeat.

Sir Sange gently patted Johanna upon her knee. "Mortality has always been simply futile and waste, rather garbage, a shameful curse by a molding creator's sickened tantrum. His error, corrected His wrong, by offering your faithless mortality as a gamely delicacy of the food chain for immortals birthed of hell. So, you begot doubt in time, as your body fails you. I can smell cancer within you, Johanna. You doubt your faith. What side does your God truly stand? He has failed you and your sister! He is not worthy of any trust or prayers!"

"No!"

"Do you want to live or die today, Johanna?" Sir Sange leaned in towards Johanna. "I could kill you with one bite and suck every ounce of blood from your body. Now, are you going to ask yourself if you'd go to heaven or hell? Damn it, woman! Spare yourself of the ongoing dichotomy between life and death and come with me, Johanna! I will bring you into immortality."

"No!"

. Johanna, I once gave you a chance to become immortal many years ago, but now I make my final and humblest sell. For, without your name, Van Helsing, you don't bear any value to me, and you will die sooner than your disease can grapple your final breath. I am thin with patience; this is an eminent bargain and a genuinely great success to the entire vampire lore. Come with me, Johanna Van Helsing."

Van Helsing suddenly grew spry of mortal hope, as she saw from the window, the sunrise upon the horizon. Shaken with doubt and light turbulence, she was torn with selfishness between becoming of the vampires and dishonoring her family or living only to die of cancer in the next few weeks.

"You must hurry," urged Sir Sange. He, too, saw a slit of sunlight on the horizon. "Come with me, Johanna!"

Back in the cockpit, one of the pilots was the captain, and he said, "It sure is quiet back there. I suspect that whatever was in the crate got out, and they killed it."

"Should we open the door and confirm that, captain?"

"Hell no," said the other pilot. "Didn't you hear the instruction Ms. Van Helsing gave us? That saint made it clear for us never to open that cabin door for any reason until we land at the base, where she has a militia awaiting. She even had the passenger door back there sealed from the outside. Only the landing crew would break the seal. And she purposely had a very thick door installed for the cabin."

"After all the ruckus with bullets and screaming a few minutes ago, your curiosity isn't eating away at you to take a peek?"

"No," answered the pilot. "She paid us to do a job. We're hired to fly this plane to Romania. Besides, haven't you seen enough movies about people who stick their noses into things they shouldn't and later get gutted? Nope, I am not the one."

"We have guns," said the captain. "What are you afraid of, man? There is no living beast that is bulletproof. Know what I'm saying? I'm responsible for the people on this flight; I have a right to know something about what's going on on my plane."

"No captain, only Johanna Van Helsing, and her money are."

The captain stood up and walked to the cabin door. He placed his ear upon it to listen. There was not a sound.

"Captain, please don't!"

"I'm not," replied the captain.

A pilot stretched his arms above his head and yawned. "Isn't that a beautiful sunrise starting beyond the horizon?"

As he turned away to acknowledge the pilot, the captain heard a loud knock on the door.

"Open this door," whispered voice. "This, I order."

"You told us never to open the door," answered the captain. "Please, Johanna, return to your seat. We have a few hours left."

She continued to knock.

"What do you need?"

Johanna seductively answered, "I saw the way you and the pilots watched me, and I wondered if maybe we can play around in the cockpit. You know, I haven't had a good time in quite some time."

"Oh my goodness," said one of the pilots, who monitored a gauge. "We're going to nail a nun!"

"Are you nuts?" The other pilot shook his head with obedience to his faith. "We'd go straight to hell over that. You'd better check yourself before you wreck yourself, dog."

"She ain't no' nun," said the captain. He didn't care about whatever game she played, as he knew there was more going on than what he had seen. "I'll be damned to miss out on getting some of that sweet action! Johanna is a dime a dozen. I'm opening this door!"

The third pilot warned, "Don't open that door! Captain, don't do it! I need the money she promised. Don't mess up our payday!"

The other pilot agreed with the captain. "Mess up our payday? I'm looking forward to messing her up and her paying extra for my sexual gifts. She ain't never been with a man like me!"

"She was fine, wasn't she?" The other pilot was convinced. "Yeah, she can't be a nun. Open the door, captain. She doesn't know who she's fucking with."

"Alright, big boys, you can turn on the Autopilot about now. We got some business to attend to." After the horny captain popped his collar and threw a mint into his mouth, he happily unlocked and opened the cabin door to invite Johanna in for a freaky tale.

"I told you," whispered Johanna, as she stood in a near spell, "to not open this door."

"Well, I just thought maybe we could have some sex."

The other pilots looked beyond the captain and Johanna. They both choked up with vomit and fear at the bloody and chunky grotesque of decapitated heads and scattered guns and knives across the aisle and chairs. Slowly, a very tall man levitated into the doorway behind Johanna. He had a raging sinisterly face, as blood drooled from the corners of his lips!

The captain noticed blood oozing from Johanna's neck! "Close the fucking door, lads!"

Sir Sange instantly extended his arm and blocked the door from being closed by the pilots! He turned to his newly converted immortal lover, and delightfully said, "You need to feed, my darling."

Suddenly guns blazed throughout the cockpit, as Johanna's newly found, painless life was unaware of her destined dismay, a looming disaster. As she went into a feeding frenzy, a pilot, whom she ripped the esophagus from, shot the dashboard and inadvertently canceled the Autopilot! Suddenly, the small plane tilted into a nosedive. It shot towards the land below at near the speed of light.

Sir Sange and Johanna magically stood firmly upon the flooring of the cockpit as all of the drained bodies rolled towards the back end of the plane with gravity. Wicked flames, hordes of smoke, and glass erupted from the dashboard, as the two vampires morphed into slimy little, hairy bats and tried to fly out any window.

Not only was the sunrise an immediate danger should they have tried to escape the plane, but the g-forces were much too intense for either Sir Sange or Johanna to handle the velocity in which they'd be ripped apart like a razor by the window seal. Suddenly, their bleached skin and blackened organs began to tear away! Together, they were violently hoisted to the back to the plane like feathers also.

Sir Sange was the comfortable assurance to thwart Johanna's non-panic, even though he was totally in fear for their inescapable demise. He ordered Johanna to morph into human form and to open the cargo hatch!

The bitter vampire knew that Johanna and his fate were not at a positive turn within the plane that dropped at a fiery and increasingly speeding rate. He too morphed into his human form and anxiously climbed down into the cargo space after Johanna. Together, they crawled into his coffin, closed its door over themselves, and held onto one another.

There was a blinding light.

Flickering and explosions continued throughout the plane wreck, as Sir Sange stood upon his only leg. He was surrounded by fire and metal fragments, body parts, and destroyed asphalt.

"No!" Sir Sange cried out in defeat to the joyous heavens once again, as he saw burning body fragments of Johanna spread all over the road. He had no will to live on, not in that skin and those clothes at least. His heart was destroyed due to love, of love, and for love.

Sir Sange dropped to his only knee, looked to the sunlight of triumph over his surrender, and suddenly burst into an ignited ball of blackened flames and smoke. The vampire again became the partial ash in which he came from and blew away into the air.

Therefore, the bloody curse of humankind would simply wait for another dumbfounded human error to resurrect him. In the case of Sir Sange, hate did beget hate, while his endless search of love would endure forever across the globe. And yes, therefore, his thirst for blood would also never go away.

By Ashaki Boelter

978-1-7358905-2-4

By Ashaki Boelter